THE RELUCTANT GUARDIAN: A REGENCY ROMANCE

LAURA BEERS

A Reluctant Guardian: A Regency Romance
By: Laura Beers

Text copyright © 2019 by Laura Beers Cover Art copyright © 2019 by Laura Beers
Cover art by Blue Water Books

All rights reserved. No part of this publication may be reproduced, stored, copied, or transmitted without the prior written permission of the copyright owner. This is a work of fiction. Names, characters, places and incidents either are the product of the author's imagination or are used fictitiously. Any resemblance to actual persons, living or dead, business establishments, events, or locales is entirely coincidental.

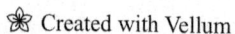 Created with Vellum

MORE ROMANCE FROM LAURA BEERS

The Beckett Files
Regency Spy Romances

Saving Shadow
A Peculiar Courtship
To Love a Spy
A Tangled Ruse
A Deceptive Bargain
The Baron's Daughter
The Unfortunate Debutante

I

England, 1812

BALDWIN, THE VISCOUNT OF MOUNTGARRET, SMILED AS HE stood on the decks of one of his merchant ships, staring out into the River Thames. The slow-moving river provided him much solace as he reflected on the past four months and how drastically his life had changed. At the beginning of the Season, he'd been heavily in debt, his estate had been in dire need of repair, and he'd been in a financial situation that would take him years to resolve... if he could resolve it at all.

Now, thanks to his cousin, Penelope, the Duchess of Blackbourne, he had become part owner of Foster Company, one of the most profitable companies in all Britain. His estate had been repaired, and all his debts were paid off.

Life is most emphatically good, he thought. No more scrounging around to survive. He was indebted to no one. He was finally free to do what his conscience dictated, and that was a wonderful, glorious feeling.

"Is everything in order, Lord Mountgarret?" the captain of the ship asked as he walked across the deck towards him.

Baldwin removed his hands from the railing and stepped back. "Yes, Captain. Everything has been loaded and secured below deck. You're free to set sail at your convenience."

"That's excellent news." The tall, older man, with white hair and a thin moustache, surveyed the ship with pride. "I anticipate we shall make good time to the East Indies."

Baldwin wrinkled his nose as the wind shifted, bringing the pungent smell of excrement from the rookeries to his nostrils. Ignoring the odor, he extended some papers towards the captain.

"Here are your official orders," he said.

Chuckling, the captain accepted the papers. "You certainly know how to run a tight ship, milord. Before you or the Duchess of Blackbourne came around, we were given our orders verbally."

"Yes, but because of our new policies, we've nearly doubled our profits from last year," Baldwin pointed out.

The captain folded the papers and tucked them into his jacket pocket. "I'm not arguing with you, milord. Your methods have made me a very rich man."

"Indeed."

"Are you sure you don't want to travel with me down to the East Indies?" the captain asked, spreading his hands out.

"Perhaps one of these days, but there is too much work to be completed here."

"By work, are you implying balls and soirées?" the captain joked.

Baldwin grinned. "I may attend the occasional theatre performance at Covent Gardens, but I'm afraid I am much too busy to mingle with the *ton* at this time."

"That is a pity."

"Is it?" he questioned. "I would much rather be in my office working than dealing with scheming mothers and their eligible daughters."

The captain smiled. "What a hardship you face, milord."

Baldwin heard a bell ringing, and the captain grew serious.

"It's time for us to depart. You'd best get off the ship, or you'll have no choice but to come with us."

"Have a safe journey," Baldwin said as he turned towards the gangway.

As he stepped onto the wooden planks, they began to sway under his feet, and he held firmly to the sides as he walked down towards the docks.

Once he stepped on solid ground, his eyes scanned the docks and all the men working. This was his life. A glorious life that he loved. He may have been born a gentleman, but he loved working in trade. He loved coming into the office every morning and meeting with clients. Many of his peers considered it beneath them to work, especially in trade, but he was grateful to have an income.

He knew all too well the stress that came with having no income. He'd been forced to sell off many of his family's artifacts just to stay out of debtor's prison. He was not ashamed of that fact, though. His father had taken out many loans before his death, and his investments never panned out, leaving Baldwin to sort out the mess. In retrospect, he doubted his father would have *ever* paid them off. He'd been a notorious gambler, who'd lost more than he ever won.

Baldwin walked towards the white warehouse that held the imported goods and his office. Another small warehouse was situated in the far corner of the large open storage space.

He stepped inside the open facility and admired the long, narrow windows spanning the length of the walls, and the countless number of well-organized crates and barrels. Long passageways broke the room into sections, and men were milling around, checking the inventory.

Striding purposefully across the warehouse, Baldwin didn't stop until he had entered his office. Penelope had done a wonderful job of decorating his space with antique furniture, paintings on the walls, and an oak desk in the center of the room.

He sat down at the desk and pulled out a ledger. He became so engrossed in balancing the books that his mind barely registered the knocking at his door.

"Come in," he ordered.

The door opened, and a short, blond-haired man, slightly on the portly side, entered. He held a bulging file in his hand.

"Lord Mountgarret, I presume?" he asked.

"You presume correctly," Baldwin replied, placing the quill next to the inkpot.

"Excellent." The man bobbed his head approvingly. "My name is Mr. Walter Baker. I am the solicitor for Mr. Thomas Barrington."

A bright smile came to Baldwin's lips at the mention of his dear childhood friend.

"Please, do come in and have a seat." He pointed at a chair in front of his desk.

Mr. Baker sat down, placing the file on the chair next to him.

"How is Mr. Barrington?" Baldwin asked, placing his forearms on the desk and leaning forward.

The solicitor's brows drew together. "You haven't heard, then?"

"Heard what?"

With a solemn expression, Mr. Baker revealed, "I regret to inform you that he and his wife passed away two weeks ago in a carriage accident."

Baldwin felt as though he had been punched in the gut. What horrific news! He had just spoken with Thomas and his wife, Anne, at the theatre a few weeks prior, and they had made plans to go fox hunting in the fall.

"I am sorry to be the bearer of bad news."

Baldwin just stared at the solicitor, hoping this was all a big misunderstanding. Thomas couldn't be dead. He was still so young!

He was silent for a long moment before he finally found himself asking, "How?"

Mr. Baker gave him a sympathetic look. "They were traveling home from the Season. A broken-down wagon had been left in the road. Their driver didn't even see it because of the dense fog that night." He grew pensive before adding, "The good news is that their two little girls were spared when the coach overturned."

Baldwin sighed in relief. "That is wonderful news!"

"I agree," Mr. Baker said, reaching over for the file. "Which is why I called on you today."

Baldwin closed his ledger and placed it to the side. He had to admit he was curious.

"You were listed in Mr. Barrington's will," Mr. Baker revealed, removing a piece of paper from the file.

"I was?" Baldwin asked, confused. Why would Thomas make provisions for him?

The solicitor nodded. "You were listed as the guardian for his two daughters, Miss Phoebe Barrington and Miss Sophia Barrington."

Baldwin shot up in his chair. "I beg your pardon?"

Seemingly unperturbed by his sudden outburst, Mr. Baker proceeded. "The girls inherited their father's estate, which is roughly valued around £55,000. In addition, they also inherited their country estate in Bath, and a London townhouse. Mr. Barrington made you a common-law guardian and the testamentary guardian, which means you are responsible for the care and nourishing of the children, as well as their property and money. It is a great honor he has bestowed upon you."

Baldwin stared at the solicitor, dumbfounded. "There must be some mistake. Mr. Barrington never asked me to be their guardian."

Reviewing the document, Mr. Baker didn't glance up as he asked, "Are you not Miss Phoebe's and Miss Sophia's godfather?"

"Yes… but…"

Mr. Baker spoke over him. "I take it that Mr. Barrington did not properly explain the duties of a godfather."

Baldwin pressed his fingers to the bridge of his nose. This couldn't be happening to him. He couldn't be the guardian to two young girls!

"Miss Phoebe is ten and Miss Sophia is eight years old," the solicitor continued.

"Is there no one else to be guardian to these two girls?" Baldwin asked, dropping his hand.

"I'm afraid not, milord," Mr. Baker replied.

He stifled a groan. "May I decline guardianship?"

The solicitor's mouth dropped in astonishment, then he hesitantly replied, "That is your right, but I hope you would reconsider it. If you do not accept guardianship, then they would become the ward of the court. The court of Chancery would then appoint a guardian for the girls."

Drat! He couldn't do that to his childhood friend's children.

"Are they old enough to be sent to boarding school?" he found himself asking.

Mr. Baker gave him a disapproving look. "No. They are much too young to be sent away to school."

Baldwin rose from his chair and stepped towards the window. What was he going to do with two young children underfoot? He still rented an apartment at Albany on Piccadilly, and no female visitors were welcome at any time, including children.

Placing his hands on the windowsill, he bent his head and sighed. He didn't know the first thing about children.

Mr. Baker broke through his musings. "If I may," he started slowly, "it might be in your best interest to hire a governess to care for the rearing of these girls. At least, until they are old enough to attend boarding school."

A governess. Of course. Why hadn't he thought of that? He would direct his housekeeper at Rumney Manor to hire a governess.

He turned back towards the solicitor. "Thank you for the suggestion, Mr. Baker. I believe I will do just that."

"Excellent," Mr. Baker said, picking up the file. "Would you like me to send them to your London townhouse?"

He shook his head. "Unfortunately, I rent an apartment at Albany."

The solicitor frowned at that piece of news. "Your country estate then?"

That didn't seem like a good alternative, either. He rarely was in residence at Rumney Manor.

"Where are Phoebe and Sophia residing now?"

"At their country estate in Bath."

Leaning back against the windowsill, he asked, "Would it be permissible to leave them there until they are old enough to go to boarding school?"

Mr. Baker blinked a few times. "I do not think that's wise. The girls need guidance and discipline."

"Is there not a household staff there?"

"There is," he began, "but unfortunately, they did not employ a governess. Mrs. Barrington saw to the girls' education."

Baldwin straightened from the windowsill and declared, "Then I shall hire a governess and send her to rear the children at their country estate."

Reaching for the file, Mr. Baker appeared frustrated. He was attempting to sound polite, but Baldwin could hear the strain in his voice.

"It would be best for the girls if you moved them to *your*

country estate, where you currently maintain a staff, and rent out their country home. It would provide them with an income, rather than drain their inheritance."

"Botheration," Baldwin muttered under his breath. He knew the solicitor was right.

The solicitor rose, walked over to the desk, and dropped the file. It landed with a thud. "I understand that becoming a guardian to Miss Phoebe and Miss Sophia came as rather a shock, but you are now responsible for two scared little girls who are grieving the loss of their parents deeply."

Baldwin had never been rendered speechless before, but he found he couldn't formulate a response. He didn't know the first thing about rearing children, especially girls. He couldn't be responsible for them. He wouldn't. There had to be another way.

"I'm afraid I will need to think it over."

Disappointment crossed Mr. Baker's features. "As you wish, milord. Kindly send a missive to my office when you have made your decision."

He watched as the solicitor left the room, then he sat down at his desk, opened the file, and found Thomas's will. Sure enough, he was listed as the guardian to Sophia and Phoebe. Why would Thomas do this to him? It was unfathomable.

Baldwin tossed the will onto the desk. He needed some advice, and there was only one person he could think of to ask.

Baldwin reined in his horse in front of Hereford Hall, the Duke of Blackbourne's townhouse. It was a stately, three-level, red brick structure, with a high four-column portico at the main entry, and large windows.

He dismounted his horse and handed off his reins to a waiting footman. His eyes scanned the pristine gardens and well-polished exterior, and he sighed. How he wanted to avoid this conversation. If only he could go back to the joy he'd felt this morning, before he was given the news.

The door to the townhouse opened, and Nicholas, the Duke of Blackbourne, stood in the doorway. His usual stoic expression was set firmly in place. "Why are you skulking around my estate?"

"I am not skulking," Baldwin countered.

"You look like you're skulking to me."

"Did Hawkins finally get fed up with you and quit?"

Nicholas's lips twitched. "No, I just happened to see you ride up, and I thought I'd greet you myself."

"*You* came to greet me?" Baldwin eyed him suspiciously as he stepped up the few stairs towards the main entrance.

"Fine," Nicholas said as he stepped to the side to allow him entry. "If you must know, Penelope is out shopping with Lady Northampton."

He stopped in the entry hall and spun back around. "You let your wife leave willingly?" He tsked.

Nicholas gave him an exasperated look. "I'm already regretting my decision to invite you into my home. I should have instructed Hawkins to deny you entry."

He glanced around the empty entry hall, looking for the butler. "Where is Hawkins?"

"He is making the necessary preparations for us to leave London, now that the Season has concluded," Nicholas shared. "We plan to retire to Brighton Hall for the fall and Lawrence Abbey for the winter."

Baldwin nodded approvingly. "I have no doubt that Penelope is excited to give you a tour of Brighton Hall. It's a Gothic castle that her father painstakingly restored before his death." A smile came to his face. "Growing up, Penelope and I would spend hours playing in the shell grotto."

"Penelope has spoken at length about her ancestral home,

and I find myself eager to tour it," Nicholas said, leading him towards his study.

As they walked into Nicholas's study, Baldwin was mindful to close the door behind him. This was a conversation that he wanted to ensure was private.

Nicholas lifted a questioning brow. "Is everything all right?"

"No," he admitted, walking further into the room. "I need your advice."

"It's about time you came to me," Nicholas said with a bob of his head. "I recommend that you fire your valet and update your wardrobe."

"I don't employ a valet."

"Clearly."

Glancing down at his fashionable blue jacket, paisley waistcoat, and tan trousers, Baldwin asked, "What's wrong with my clothing?"

"If you have to ask, then you are in worse trouble than I thought," Nicholas replied with mirth in his voice.

"Enough. I did not come to you about my clothing."

"Pity." Nicholas stepped over to the drink cart and took the stopper off the decanter. "Then why did you come?" He poured two drinks and extended one towards Baldwin.

Stepping forward, Baldwin accepted the drink and sipped it. He brought his glass down and said, "I just received the most horrific news."

Nicholas grew serious. "Which was?"

"My childhood friend, Mr. Thomas Barrington, and his wife, died in a carriage accident," he revealed, his voice hitching.

Reaching out, Nicholas placed a comforting hand on his shoulder. "My condolences for your loss."

"Thank you."

The duke withdrew his hand. "Were you still close to Mr. Barrington and his wife?"

"Thomas and I were roommates at Eton College and then at

Oxford," he shared. "We both studied to be barristers and applied to the Inns of Court."

"Were you not called up to the bar?" Nicholas asked.

Baldwin shook his head. "There were a few reasons I decided not to pursue law. The foremost being the compounding debts my father left me to deal with. I needed to focus on increasing my income at Rumney Manor." He walked over to a settee and sat down. "But Thomas tried cases in court."

Nicholas came to sit next to him. "I truly am sorry for your loss. I know what it's like to lose a friend."

"I know you do," Baldwin stated. "I have no doubt you've lost many comrades while serving as a captain in His Majesty's Royal Navy."

Nicholas's eyes grew pensive. "I've lost too many to count."

"I watched Thomas marry Anne," Baldwin said, bringing the glass to his lips, "and I was present at each one of his daughters' christenings." He frowned. "I was supposed to visit his country estate in November for the hunt."

"Is there anything we can do to help you?"

He sighed. "Frankly, it hasn't sunk in yet. I'm still hoping to hear that it was a grand mistake."

"No one can prepare you for the death of a loved one," Nicholas remarked.

"That's true," Baldwin replied, placing his empty glass on the table.

A solemn, reflective silence descended over them as Baldwin attempted to gather strength for what he knew was going to be a most difficult conversation.

"Thomas's solicitor came by my office today to inform me of his death," he started.

"That was nice of him."

Baldwin pursed his lips together. His visit had not been 'nice'. He decided to just say what needed to be said and be done with it.

"Thomas listed me as the guardian of his two daughters."

Nicholas's brow lifted. "How old are his daughters?"

"Miss Phoebe is ten and Miss Sophia is eight," he shared, hoping he remembered that correctly.

To his surprise, and great annoyance, Nicholas leaned his head back and laughed.

Baldwin rose from his chair and stepped to the window. He attempted to ignore his friend's laughter as he stared out over the gardens.

"I'm sorry," Nicholas said as his laughter faded. "Did you just say that you are the guardian to two young girls?" The humor in his voice was undeniable.

"I did."

"You are one unlucky bloke," the duke stated, shaking his head.

Baldwin placed his hand on the window frame and leaned forward. "I am aware of that fact."

"Are you bringing your charges to Rumney Manor?"

"Do you think I should?"

He heard Nicholas rise from his seat. "I do. Where else would they go?"

Turning back to face him, Baldwin said, "I am debating about turning down the guardianship of the girls."

"I see," Nicholas muttered as he stepped over to the drink cart and put his glass down.

"What do I know about taking care of two little girls?" he asked.

Nicholas watched him for a long moment, disappointment clearly on his features. "You would dishonor your friend's legacy by turning down the guardianship of his greatest treasures?"

"You don't understand…"

Nicholas spoke over him. "I do understand. I inherited guardianship of your cousin, Penelope, and I never once considered turning it down. In fact, I was wholly unprepared to have an eighteen-year-old girl as my ward."

"It's different."

"Is it?"

"You married her!" he shouted. "I'd say it worked out rather splendidly for you."

The duke let out a slight huff. "These girls need you. They just lost their mother and father. They are alone in the world."

"Why me?"

"Why *not* you?" Nicholas challenged. "It's evident that your friend trusted you and assumed he could rely on you."

Tossing up his hands, Baldwin proclaimed, "I can't care for two little girls! I just can't."

"Then you're not the man I thought you were," Nicholas replied, his words piercing Baldwin's heart.

He let out a deep, heartfelt sigh, knowing that his friend was right. He had no choice. He must take guardianship of the two girls.

"Thomas's solicitor suggested I could hire a governess to raise the children," he shared slowly.

"That's a good start," Nicholas agreed, "but you will need to be more involved in their lives than just ensuring they receive a proper education."

He ran his hand through his hair. "I have no idea how to raise two girls."

"You'll figure it out."

"I wish I had your confidence."

The duke smiled. "Penelope will be thrilled to discover that she'll have two girls to spoil."

"Indeed." Baldwin started for the door. "I will ask Thomas's solicitor to send the girls to Rumney Manor."

Nicholas nodded approvingly. "I think that would be wise."

Baldwin's hand had just touched the door handle when the

duke continued. "If you need anything, Penelope and I are always willing to help."

"Thank you," he replied, opening the door. "I might take you up on that."

"Good luck," Nicholas said.

As Baldwin exited Hereford Hall, he knew in his heart that he was making the right decision, but that didn't make it any easier. What did he know about raising girls? He would need to ensure a governess was hired, and quickly. But where would he find one on such short notice?

2

A BRIGHT SMILE GRACED EMELINE WARREN'S FACE AS SHE raced her horse through the woodlands surrounding Cairnwood Hall, her ancestral home. Tall birch trees lined both sides of the path as she kept herself low in the saddle, urging her horse to run faster. A deer popped its head up as she rode by, lazily chewing shrubbery, making no effort to run from her.

Some of her brown hair had escaped her chignon and was flowing scandalously behind her. Up ahead was a trickling stream, and she slowed her horse's gait. Once she arrived at the stream, Emeline reined in her horse, dismounted, and led her grey gelding to drink. She listened to the birds warbling overhead and sighed contentedly. These woods had always provided her with solace and peace, away from her controlling and demeaning stepmother.

Pulling a dark green leaf from a square stem, she plopped it into her mouth and savored the peppermint flavor. How she loved these woodlands. She and her mother had spent countless hours scouring the grounds for herbs. Her mother had been insistent that she become proficient in botany, so she could always help those less fortunate.

She heard the sound of pounding hooves in the distance, then saw Harry Garvey breaking through the trees.

The tall, weathered-faced, lead groomsman pulled back on the reins and said, "I don't know how you keep beating me, Miss Warren."

"Perhaps it's time for you to admit that the apprentice has finally become the master," she replied jovially.

"Never," he declared with a solemn face, but she detected the humor in his voice.

She ran her gloved hand down the length of her horse's neck. "I fear your old age is making you soft," she teased.

He huffed as he dismounted. "I am not even forty."

Gasping, she replied, "You're that old?"

Harry chuckled as he led his horse to the stream. "It's good to have you home, miss."

"It's good to be back," she admitted. "This past Season was exhausting."

"Poor Miss Warren," he joked.

Emeline smiled at her dear friend before revealing, "Priscilla was relentless. Every night, she had something scheduled for us to do. Whether it was a ball, soirée, or the theatre."

"And yet, you didn't ensnare a husband." Harry smirked.

She stepped away from her horse and looked up at the canopy of trees. "Don't remind me of that fact," she groaned. "Priscilla is still fuming that I didn't accept Sir Thomas Rowling's offer."

"Your stepmother is just looking out for you," Harry pressed.

She looked at him in disbelief. "Not if she wanted me to marry Sir Thomas."

"If you don't mind me asking, what exactly was wrong with Sir Thomas?"

Emeline took a moment to mull over her answer. "He wasn't completely awful," she found herself admitting.

"That sounded convincing," Harry mocked.

She decided to tell him the truth... the partial truth. "The issue was his thick moustache."

"You rejected him because of his moustache?" Harry sounded skeptical.

Nodding, she shared, "One evening, I found myself sitting next to him during dinner, and he kept getting crumbs stuck into his moustache."

"Moustaches can be shaved," Harry said with a knowing brow.

Sighing, she gently rested her head on her horse's neck. "I couldn't imagine spending the rest of my life with Sir Thomas. He spoke to me only about polite topics."

"Was that so bad?"

"I don't want to marry a man that asks me if my embroidery skills are improving."

Harry chuckled. "Did Sir Thomas ask you that?"

"Yes, as did Lord Cornwall and Lord Weatherpool."

Harry grew solemn. "That *is* a valid question. If you aren't accomplished at needlework, then you have failed as a gentlewoman."

"You sound just like Priscilla." She kicked at a rock near the stream and was gratified to see it take flight. "I'm not even sure if I want to marry. Is it so wrong that I want to be free to lead my own life, without the constraints of a husband?"

"Then don't marry."

"I can't." She frowned. "As Priscilla has continually reminded me, Juliet can't have a Season until I have entered a courtship."

"But your step-sister isn't even eighteen yet."

"That doesn't seem to matter to Priscilla or Juliet." She ran her hand down her blue riding habit. "Juliet has all but demanded that I must marry so she can have a Season next year."

Adjusting the reins in his hands, Harry asked, "What does your father say?"

"According to Priscilla, he has ordered me to marry immediately," she shared.

"Do you believe that?"

She shook her head. "I do not, but I haven't seen my father in over eight months. He's been buying and selling commodities in the West Indies."

"Well, you may find a handsome gentleman in the country this fall," he said, wagging his brows.

Laughing, she replied, "I daresay that is impossible living in Bristol. There is not one gentleman younger than my father in the surrounding areas."

"Now you're just being too selective." Harry winked to let her know he was teasing. "I believe we've dallied long enough. I would hate to cut into your embroidery time."

Walking over, Harry intertwined his fingers and assisted her up onto her side saddle. He placed his hand on her horse's neck and said, "You're still young…"

"I'm nearly twenty-one," she contended, speaking over him.

"That is still young to me." He smiled. "As I was saying, trust your instincts when it comes to finding a husband. There are good men out there, but you must sort through a lot of scoundrels first."

"Scoundrels?" she asked, amused.

He stepped back. "Trust me. I know what I am speaking of."

"I do, completely."

"Good." Harry mounted his horse. "I'll see you back at the estate," he said as he kicked his horse into a run.

With a laugh, Emeline followed suit and raced her horse back towards the estate. They had just broken through the trees when she saw a black-crested coach in the courtyard. She recognized the crest as belonging to the Earl of Mortain. She let out a groan.

Why had *he* come to call?

She turned her horse towards the stable and decided to put the aging earl out of her mind. Clearly, he'd come to call on her stepmother and not her, which was a relief. The last time Earl Mortain had come to call, he'd spent the entire hour talking about himself. She had learned in great detail that he was an avid hunter and, as a youth, would occasionally engage in fisticuffs with his friend.

Emeline reined in her horse in the stable yard, and a groomsman ran out to meet her. While she dismounted, Jonathon said, "Mrs. Warren requested your presence in the drawing room."

"Did my stepmother say why my presence is required?"

Jonathon shook his head. "No, Miss Warren."

"Thank you for relaying the message," she said kindly.

As she walked the short distance to the estate, she took a moment to fix her hair and smooth out her riding gown. The last thing she wanted to do was to meet with Lord Mortain. He was pretentious and boring.

The door to the estate opened, and the butler stood aside to grant her entry. "How was your ride, miss?"

"It went well."

Mr. Grant arched an eyebrow. "Did you beat Harry to the stream?"

"How could you even ask that question?" she replied with a playful smile.

Chuckling, he tilted his head towards the drawing room. "Mrs. Warren has been waiting for nearly an hour for your arrival. You'd best hurry."

She took a step closer to him and lowered her voice. "When did Lord Mortain arrive?"

"About thirty minutes ago."

As she turned to leave, Mr. Grant ordered, "Wait, young lady." He reached over and pulled something out of her hair. "Your stepmother would be furious if she saw you had a leaf in your hair."

"Thank you," she said gratefully before moving towards the drawing room.

Her stepmother, a handsome woman with a slim face and high cheekbones, greeted her as she stepped into the room.

"There you are, my child," Mrs. Warren said tersely as she rose gracefully from the settee. "Lord Mortain was gracious enough to come calling this afternoon." She walked over to her and leaned closer. "You will behave. Understood?"

Emeline gave her stepmother a brief nod, fighting the impulse to run in the opposite direction. There was no point in arguing with her on this topic. With any luck, the earl would depart shortly.

Lord Mortain had risen when she walked in, and he was waiting for her to approach him.

She stepped closer to him and dipped into a curtsey. "Lord Mortain," she murmured respectfully.

As the earl presented her with a bow, Emeline took a moment to study the man. He was heavy-set, with a round face, and appeared to be in his early fifties. The salt-and-pepper hair, which could only be considered sparse, was combed over the top of his head, and blended awkwardly with too-long, white hair running over his ears.

Shaking herself from her perusal when she realized the earl and her stepmother were watching her expectedly, Emeline forced a smile to her lips.

"Miss Warren, you are looking especially lovely today," he practically purred.

"You are most kind, my lord," she replied. "I apologize if I've kept you waiting."

Lord Mortain smiled, revealing a row of yellow, crooked teeth. "You have nothing to apologize for. I hope that you enjoyed your walk."

"I actually…"

Her stepmother interjected, "Daily walks are vital for a

young woman's complexion, assuming she always wears a bonnet or a straw hat."

The earl nodded approvingly. "I agree. Protection from the sun is most important for women's delicate constitutions."

"You are most wise, my lord," Mrs. Warren acknowledged in a light, airy tone.

In response, the earl puffed out his chest in pride as Emeline resisted the urge to frown at her stepmother's blatant attempts at flattery.

"Emeline," her stepmother began, "why don't you pour a cup of tea for his lordship?"

"As you wish, stepmother."

She sat down next to Juliet on the settee and reached for the teapot on the tray in front of her. Her stepsister gave her an icy glance before sliding further away from her on the settee.

Lowering himself onto his chair, Lord Mortain continued to watch her closely. She filled his teacup and extended it towards him.

He accepted the cup, and his gloved fingers brushed up against hers. "Thank you, my dear," he said in a tone that caused repulsion to crawl up her spine.

"Lord Mortain has been sharing stories about grouse hunting," Mrs. Warren stated from her seat.

"How exciting," Emeline replied in a dry tone. "I believe last time he shared stories about fox hunting, and the ten hounds he bred specifically for the hunt."

Her stepmother cast her a warning look, but her sarcastic comment was lost on Lord Mortain. "You have an excellent memory, Miss Warren," he declared. "I also have eight hunters, which are horses bred for the hunt."

"Eight," she repeated, feigning interest. "That's quite impressive."

Lord Mortain sipped his tea with a slurp before lowering the cup to his lap. "Now that the dreadful London Season is over,

Society will retire to the country to shoot birds during the autumn and hunt foxes during the winter," he shared. "I prefer hunting over mingling with the *ton*. Although, I fear it *is* rather similar." He chuckled, amused by his own joke.

Mrs. Warren let out a laugh. "That was rather witty."

"It was, wasn't it?" he replied.

Oh bother, Emeline thought, as her eyes drifted towards the window. She would much rather be outside on a day like this than inside entertaining a pompous lord.

The earl's words broke through her musings. "Don't you agree, Miss Warren?"

"I beg your pardon," she said, bringing her gaze back towards the earl.

With a frown on his lips, he stated, "I said it would be a fine day to take a stroll in the gardens."

"Oh, yes," she agreed.

"Then, it's settled," Earl Mortain proclaimed, rising and placing his teacup onto the table.

"Settled, my lord?" she asked.

"We shall take a stroll in the gardens together." He extended his pudgy hand towards her.

She shrank back and attempted to think of a reason to decline. *Any reason.* But not one was forthcoming.

"Lord Mortain is honoring you with this gesture, Emeline," her stepmother encouraged in a tense tone.

Juliet leaned closer and nudged her with her shoulder. "Go," she hissed next to her ear.

Tentatively, Emeline reached out and placed her hand in his. He helped her rise and smiled at her. She couldn't say with certainty why his smile repulsed her, but it most assuredly did. It was through sheer willpower that she resisted the urge to jerk her hand away from his.

Lord Mortain tucked her hand into the crook of his arm. "Will you lead me to the gardens, Miss Warren?"

She forced a smile onto her face. "Of course, Lord Mortain."

As she led him towards the rear of the estate, he glanced over at her and said, "Mrs. Warren informed me that you received a thorough education at Miss Bell's Finishing School."

"I did."

"May I ask what languages you speak?"

"French, Italian, and German."

He nodded approvingly. "And which instruments do you play?"

As they stepped out into the well-manicured gardens, she replied, "The pianoforte and harp."

"Very good," he murmured. "Are you well-read?"

Knowing the answer he sought, she replied, "I only read books on piety and cookery."

Lord Mortain stopped and turned to face her. "Excellent. I cannot abide a woman that reads poetry or political books."

"Nor I," she admonished, stifling a smile. "There is nothing worse than a woman who thinks on her own. Heaven forbid that she should join the men in a lively debate on politics!"

"I concur," Lord Mortain agreed with a bob of his head.

"Somehow, I knew you would," she remarked, her eyes darting towards the well-groomed shrubs and brightly colored flowers.

Lord Mortain cleared his throat, drawing back her attention. "As you know, my wife died four months ago, and I have been quite lonely at my estate."

A feeling of dread washed over her. "I understand," she said, hoping to change the topic of conversation.

"You do?"

She nodded. "After my mother died, I felt lonely, so my father brought me home a dog."

"A dog." He gave her a baffled look.

"Yes, a dog," she confirmed. "Since you already have ten dogs, you may want to consider bringing one inside with you."

With a furrowed brow, Lord Mortain stated, "My dogs are bred for hunting, not socialization."

"Pity," she said as she continued strolling the gardens. With any luck, Lord Mortain would take the hint and not broach the marriage subject again.

She wasn't that lucky.

"I was thinking more along the lines of a wife to keep me company," he shared, matching her stride.

"That's a brilliant idea," she said, keeping her gaze straight ahead.

"It is?" he asked, confused.

She nodded. "There are many women in London that would be thrilled to be courted by an earl of your caliber."

"Just in London?" He placed his hand on her arm and turned her to face him.

With a puzzled look on her face, she said, "I would imagine you are looking for someone who is of a similar age as your late wife."

Lord Mortain frowned. "I was hoping for someone younger than my Ethel."

"Oh," she said, pressing her lips together. "I suppose I can put together a list of women of marriageable age for you. Would that assist in your search?"

He stared at her for a long moment, then said, "There seems to be some confusion on your part. I am attempting to offer for *you*."

"For *me*?" she asked, feigning surprise. "But I'm nowhere near Lady Mortain's age."

"I know. As I said, I was hoping for someone younger."

She took a step back, creating more distance between them. "Your daughter, Lady Marianne, and I are the same age."

"Is that a problem?" he asked, taking a step closer to her.

Placing her hand up, she rested it on his chest. "Yes, it's a problem."

He glanced down at her hand. "Age is relative," he said in a flirtatious tone.

"No, age is a number. And I refuse to marry someone who is old enough to be my father."

Lord Mortain's expression grew defiant. "I didn't anticipate this refusal. This will be an advantageous match for you, since you are only the daughter of a merchant."

"I am also the granddaughter of a baron," she reminded him.

"That means very little," he scoffed. "I'm offering you the opportunity to become the Countess of Mortain."

Removing her hand from his chest, Emeline replied, "I thank you for the great honor you have bestowed upon me, but I am not interested in marrying you."

"You're not?" he asked in a surprised tone.

"No," she said with a shake of her head.

He scowled. "You would rather remain a spinster than marry me?"

"I am hardly a spinster, my lord!" she declared, straightening her shoulders.

"You just completed your third Season, and you have received no offers," he pointed out.

"That's not true."

He put his arms up and asked, "If that is not the case, then why are you not married?"

"I rejected the offers."

"Pardon?" he asked, taking a step closer to her. "Did you just say 'offers'?"

She tilted her chin. "I did."

"And you rejected them all?" he asked in disbelief.

"I did."

"Were these advantageous offers?"

"They were."

His eyes narrowed slightly. "Either you are lying, or you're a bigger fool than I thought."

Taking a deep breath to calm her nerves, Emeline said, "Lord Mortain, I understand you are upset…"

"Upset?" He shook his head. "No. I'm just surprised that the daughter of a merchant has rejected my suit. I daresay you will be hard-pressed to find anyone titled who is willing to marry you now."

"I am not interested in a title, Lord Mortain," she responded, trying to ignore the sting of his sharp tongue. "What I am searching for is someone to love me."

"Bah!" he shouted. "The word love is overly dramatized. You are setting yourself up for failure, my dear. Love does not exist in our circles."

"Then so be it," she declared. "I refuse to settle for anything less."

Lord Mortain glanced back at the estate. "If you will excuse me, I find I have a sudden urge to walk back to my estate… alone."

She gave him a weak smile. "I will inform your driver."

"Thank you," he said, watching her closely. "If you change your mind, I would still be willing to marry you, Miss Warren."

"Even after everything that has been spoken between us?" she asked, surprised.

He nodded. "I would be good to you. I would dress you in the finest gowns, drape you in expensive jewels, and I promise that you would socialize in the highest circles amongst the *ton*."

"Thank you," she began, "but I'm looking for more than just material possessions."

"I don't fully understand your logic, but I find I must accept it." He bowed and started walking down the paved path out of the gardens.

Emeline sighed as she watched his retreating figure, hoping she had not offended him. She turned back toward the estate and wished she could escape as easily as Lord Mortain had. Priscilla was sure to be furious that she rejected the wealthy earl's suit.

THE RELUCTANT GUARDIAN: A REGENCY ROMANCE

Sitting at the head of the dining table, Priscilla fumed. "I can't believe you rejected an earl's suit. Are you mad?"

"No, stepmother, I am not mad," Emeline calmly said for the tenth time since they'd sat down to eat supper.

"Then why would you reject his suit?"

She sighed. "Lord Mortain is the same age as Father."

"So?" she retorted. "He is an earl. You would have been a countess."

Reaching for her teacup, Emeline wanted to be done with this frustrating conversation. Priscilla had refused to let the matter drop and had been yelling at her since Lord Mortain walked away from the estate, hours ago.

Juliet spoke up from her side of the table. "Why are you being so selfish, Emeline?"

"I beg your pardon?" she asked, lifting her brow.

"If you had only agreed to marry Lord Mortain, then I would finally have been able to have my Season next year. Don't you care about me at all?" she pouted, sounding more like a spoiled child than a seventeen-year-old young lady.

"I do," she said, hoping that sounded somewhat convincing, "but I could not marry Lord Mortain."

"But he is an earl," Juliet contended.

She took a sip of her drink. "Then, why don't *you* marry Lord Mortain?"

Juliet's mouth dropped open. "You cannot be serious. He is much too old for me."

"We're only three years apart," Emeline pointed out.

With a smug smile, Juliet said, "Yes, but everyone knows that you are destined for spinsterhood."

"Everyone?" she asked innocently, returning her teacup to the saucer. "May I ask who you have spoken to?"

Juliet's face went slack. "Well, just mother."

"But you said 'everyone', which leads me to believe you spoke to multiple people on my behalf," Emeline pressed.

With a scrunched nose, Juliet stated, "It's an expression."

"Is it? I haven't heard it before."

"I'm quite sure you've heard it before."

She shook her head. "No. This is the first time."

"Truly?"

Priscilla huffed. "Stop tormenting your sister, Emeline."

"Stepsister," Juliet and Emeline said in unison.

Priscilla turned her attention towards Emeline. "You've had three Seasons to find a husband, and you've failed. I have decided that you shall take Lord Mortain up on his offer of marriage."

"Absolutely not!" she exclaimed.

"You have no choice in the matter," Priscilla pressed. "I will post the banns, and you shall be married in three weeks' time."

Juliet gave her a smug smile as she crossed her arms over her chest.

"You can't do this!" Emeline cried.

Leaning back in her chair, Priscilla considered her for a moment, then said, "For the past three Seasons, I've watched you reject offer after offer for frivolous reasons. You won't receive a better offer than the one from Lord Mortain."

"Because he is an earl?"

"Precisely," Priscilla replied. "That will raise our social status amongst the *ton*, which will help Juliet's prospects next Season."

Emeline stared at her stepmother in disbelief. "So, you would sacrifice me to secure a better marriage offer for Juliet."

"You would be a countess," Priscilla stated as if she was a simpleton. "What more could you possibly want?"

Placing her napkin onto the table, she declared, "I want to fall in love!"

"Love does not exist," Priscilla said. "You have filled your mind with fantastical nonsense."

An uncomfortable thought came to her mind. "Do you not love my father?"

Priscilla visibly stiffened. "We get along."

"Is that why Father is never home?" she asked curiously.

Shoving back her chair, Priscilla rose and snapped, "How dare you! You have no right to speak to me this way! I am your stepmother."

"I apologize. I meant no disrespect," Emeline replied, lowering her gaze. She knew better than to antagonize her stepmother.

Priscilla placed her hands onto the table. "I have tried my best with you, but you're an impossible case. You may have attended a prestigious finishing school, but your proper education is severely lacking." She leaned closer. "I've even caught you reading books on philosophy in the library. You know those subjects are prohibited to women."

"Philosophy?" Juliet repeated as she looked at her reflection in the curvature of a spoon. "How can you even understand what the men are trying to say?"

Emeline glanced over at her blonde-haired stepsister. She was a beautiful young woman with porcelain-like skin, straight nose, and full lips, but the poor thing wasn't very clever. In fact, she was intolerably stupid.

"Those subjects are only forbidden if we allow them to be," Emeline argued, ignoring her stepsister's comment.

"What radical nonsense!" Priscilla objected. "I am finished with this conversation. You will marry Lord Mortain."

"I will not."

With a dismissive wave of her hand, Priscilla declared, "My mind is made up. You have no choice in the matter, not anymore."

"You can't do that!"

Priscilla smiled cruelly at her. "I am your stepmother, dear. I only have your best interest at heart."

"Regardless, I refuse to marry Lord Mortain!" Emeline declared.

Reaching for her teacup, Juliet remarked, "I, for one, can't seem to understand why Lord Mortain would want to marry someone as plain as you. You would think he would desire a more attractive wife."

"That was a cruel thing to say, even for you," Emeline replied.

Juliet took a sip of her tea. "It was merely an observation."

Taking her napkin off her lap, Emeline placed it onto the table and said, "I find that my appetite has left me."

Priscilla nodded approvingly. "That is for the best. You have been looking rather plump lately."

Without responding to that ridiculous comment, Emeline rose and hurried out of the dining room with her head held high. She didn't want her stepmother to know that her last comment had hurt her deeply.

Rather than adjourn to her bedchamber, Emeline raced out the main door and didn't stop until she arrived at the stables. She stepped inside and took a deep breath, staring at the lighted sconces on the wall, illuminating the stable.

"What did she do?" Harry asked, stepping out of one of the stalls.

"Priscilla is attempting to force me to marry Lord Mortain by posting the banns," she replied, her voice hitching.

"I see," he said in a steely tone. "What are you going to do?"

Removing a brush from the wall, Emeline walked over to her horse's stall and stepped inside. She started brushing her horse down.

"I refuse to marry him," she responded resolutely, "but my reputation will be in tatters if I don't go through with the wedding."

"Then so be it," Harry said resolutely. "There are worse things than a tattered reputation."

"You're right. A loveless marriage would be one of those." She stilled her brushing, looking thoughtful. "I miss my mother." Tears came to her eyes. "I miss her every single day."

Placing his forearms on the stall door, Harry leaned in. "I know, Em."

"You haven't called me that since I was a little girl," she remarked, turning to face him with a sad half-smile.

In response, he just smiled tenderly at her.

A comfortable silence descended over them. After a moment, she asked, "Do you think my father is happy with Priscilla?"

Harry sighed. "I don't know. He never used to travel so much when your mother was alive."

Emeline continued to brush her horse. "That was my thought as well. I miss my father, too." She made no effort to wipe the tears that were now flowing down her cheeks. "He abandoned me with Priscilla and her awful daughter."

"Your father did what he thought was best for you when he married Mrs. Warren four years ago," Harry attempted.

She shook her head. "No, he did what he thought was best for *him*. He didn't care what happened to me."

"That's not true," Harry contended.

Turning to face the lead groomsman, she declared, "How would I know that? He married a woman that hates me. She criticizes me at every opportunity and now is attempting to force me to marry a man that is my father's age."

"Mrs. Warren is only trying…"

She cut him off. "Don't," she challenged. "Don't you dare defend her."

Frowning, Harry said, "She may drag you along to every ball, soirée, and social gathering in all of London, but she can't physically force you to marry Lord Mortain. Last I checked, that's still against the law in England."

"Perhaps you're right," she admitted reluctantly.

"Of course, I'm right." He put his hand out for the brush.

Emeline extended it towards him. "At least, in two months' time, I shall turn twenty-one, and I'll inherit my grandmother's estate. It will provide me with enough funds to move out of here and rent a home of my own."

"You would leave your ancestral estate?"

"I would," she said. "Frankly, I don't know how much longer I can abide being around Priscilla and her witless daughter."

He watched her with concern in his eyes. "Is it truly that awful for you?"

"It is."

Removing his arms from the stall door, Harry stepped back. "It shall all work out in the end, Em."

"I don't know how," she replied honestly as she stepped out of the stall.

As Harry hung the brush back on the wall, he said, "I've never known you to give up so easily."

"It's more about being practical."

He smiled. "Perhaps you could go into the kitchen and ask Mrs. Jenkins to heat you up some of that chocolate you like to drink."

"Chocolate doesn't solve everything."

"Doesn't it?" he asked with a grin.

She found herself returning his smile. "All right. It may solve most things."

"Now, off with you," he said. "I shall see you tomorrow for our early morning ride."

Emeline nodded her acknowledgement and headed towards the servant's entrance of the estate. Harry was right that Priscilla couldn't force her into an arranged marriage. Furthermore, he most assuredly was right about chocolate. That drink could solve almost any problem!

3

EMELINE COULDN'T HELP BUT SMILE AS SHE APPROACHED Cairnwood Hall after her morning ride with Harry. She dismounted and handed off her reins to a waiting footman.

The door to the estate opened, and Mr. Grant greeted her with a warm smile. "How was your ride, miss?"

Her smile grew. "It was delightful."

Closing the door, the butler lowered his voice. "Mrs. Warren is requesting your presence in her bedchamber."

That news caused her smile to vanish. "Drat," she muttered under her breath.

In response, Mr. Grant lifted an eyebrow, but thankfully didn't comment.

"I suppose I must get this over with." She moved across the entry hall, which had columns framing the doors and a mural painted on the ceiling. A large staircase led up to the second level, where the bedchambers were located.

Her feet felt like they were made of lead as she walked down the hall towards her stepmother's bedchamber. She had no doubt that Priscilla would lecture her about why she should marry Lord

Mortain, and there would be no speaking, arguing, or cajoling. In fact, she wouldn't be able to get a single word in, she was sure.

When her father had first informed her about offering for Priscilla, she'd been overjoyed. Her stepmother had seemed so kind and loving, but that had changed the moment they'd married. Priscilla became controlling, cynical, and she had a nasty temper. It was no wonder her father started taking extended business trips, leaving her behind.

She heard Juliet's whining voice down the hall. "Mother!"

Emeline shook her head. She couldn't begin to understand her stepsister. Juliet was beautiful, but she lacked wits in so many regards. She enjoyed talking about two things: complaining about her life and bragging how she was going to snag herself a rich lord.

Emeline had no doubt that Juliet would marry well, considering she had an alluring figure and a beautiful face. There were many members of the peerage that were looking for just that. But she worried whether her stepsister would ever be truly happy with her lot in life.

Up ahead, Emeline saw that the door to her stepmother's bedchamber was slightly open, and she heard muffled noises coming from within. She was about to make her presence known when she heard Juliet huff, "She's on her morning ride."

Even though she knew it was rude to eavesdrop, Emeline stepped quietly closer to the door and peered in. Her stepmother was sitting at her dressing table, and Juliet was sitting on the bed. Both of their backs were to her, and they were unaware that the door was ajar.

"What an insipid girl," Priscilla muttered as she placed some lotion on her arms.

Juliet nodded. "All Emeline cares about is riding her horse and reading her boring books."

"Exactly. She is a bluestocking, my dear. You'd be wise to remember to avoid reading books."

"I do," Juliet answered proudly. "Perhaps you should send her back to Miss Bell's Finishing School in Bath. That would rid us of her."

"She has already had a Season…"

Juliet spoke over her. "Three Seasons, Mother!" she cried. "Three long Seasons."

"I am well aware of that fact, considering I am the one that chaperoned her."

"How awful for you."

Priscilla picked up a brush from the dressing table. "It matters not. She shall be married off in three weeks' time, and we shall be done with her."

"What if she refuses to marry Lord Mortain?" Juliet asked in her usual whiny tone.

Brushing her long, greying hair, her stepmother replied, "She has no choice."

"But she seemed adamant last night…"

"I've already devised a plan," Priscilla said, cutting her off. "Until she agrees to marry Lord Mortain, she will be locked in her bedchamber."

Emeline stifled the gasp that came to her lips. Would her stepmother be that cruel?

"Emeline is quite stubborn. What if she keeps refusing?"

Waving her hand dismissively in front of her, Priscilla declared, "Then she shall die in her room, for all I care."

"You can't be serious?" Juliet asked. "Won't her father be furious if he discovers that you locked her in her bedchamber?"

"Frankly, I don't care. He left me to contend with that horrible child."

Juliet nodded. "No wonder her father is always away on business. He can't abide his own daughter and her ugly face."

Emeline bit her lower lip, willing herself not to cry. Why would Juliet say such cruel things about her?

"She's not completely unfortunate to look at with her high

cheekbones, tapering chin, and small nose," Priscilla remarked, "but she pales in comparison to you, my dear."

"Emeline is just jealous of me," Juliet declared.

"Of course, she is. After all, you are destined to be the 'incomparable' during the next Season, assuming Emeline is out of the way."

"It's true," Juliet agreed. "Perhaps I shall marry a duke."

"I should say so." Placing the brush on the table, Priscilla shifted in her chair towards Juliet. "If in five days' time, Emeline still refuses to marry Lord Mortain, then I've already found two doctors that will declare her mad."

"But Emeline isn't mad, is she?"

"In order to send her to Bedlam, two doctors must attest to her 'hysteria'."

Emeline could hear the smile on Juliet's face when she said, "I've heard that patients are chained to their beds, and you can pay to see them."

"That practice stopped nearly thirty years ago," Priscilla remarked dryly. "We used to pay a shilling for admission, and we would laugh at the residents in their cells. For an extra six-pence, you could purchase a long stick to poke them."

"That sounds awful."

Priscilla shrugged her shoulders. "What do we care? No one cares for Emeline, not even her own father."

Hearing enough, Emeline cautiously stepped back and away from the door. How could her stepmother be so callous as to just discard her in such a horrendous fashion? And it wasn't true about her father! He loved her. She was sure of it.

Picking up her skirts, she raced towards the main entrance, ignoring the curious glances from the servants.

Mr. Grant opened the door and asked, "Are you all right, miss?"

She didn't bother to slow down as she replied, "My stepmother is awful."

Emeline didn't stop running until she arrived at the stables. A few groomsmen tipped their heads politely at her, but her eyes scanned the stalls for Harry.

"Harry!" she shouted urgently.

Coming out of a stall nearby, Harry rushed over to her when he saw the distress on her features. "What is it, Miss Warren?" he asked, his eyes roaming her face with concern.

"Priscilla plans to declare me mad if I don't marry Lord Mortain," she rushed out.

"But you aren't mad!"

Tears came to her eyes. "It doesn't matter. Priscilla has already found two doctors that are willing to testify to my 'hysteria'. She intends to send me to Bedlam."

Reaching out, Harry grabbed her arm and led her into his small office. He dropped her arm and closed the door.

"Start from the beginning."

She moved slowly to a small, rickety wooden chair and sat down. "I overheard Priscilla telling Juliet that she plans to lock me in my bedchamber until I consent to marry Lord Mortain. If I still refuse after five days, then she will summon the doctors and declare me mad."

"What doctor would declare you mad?"

She shrugged one shoulder. "I don't know, but Priscilla said she already found two of them."

"If what you are saying is true, we need to get you far away from Mrs. Warren."

"I agree. But where can I go?" she asked. "I won't be able to access my inheritance for another two months."

Harry stared out the window for a long moment before he finally said, "I have an idea." Coming around the desk, he opened a drawer and removed a piece of paper. "My sister is the housekeeper at Lord Mountgarret's estate, Rumney Manor, in Cardiff. She lives in a cottage on the property, and she will keep your secret."

He bent his head and reached for a quill. As he wrote, he shared, "If you remained in Bristol, Priscilla would find you. But I daresay she would never think of looking in Cardiff for you."

Emeline rose. "I shall depart at once."

"You cannot travel on your own," Harry stated, rising. He walked over to the door, opened it and shouted, "Jonathon!"

A dark-haired, burly young man came rushing over to the door. "Yes, Mr. Garvey."

Harry ushered him into the room and closed the door. "I have an assignment for you, and it is of the utmost urgency."

Jonathon puffed out his chest in pride as he met the lead groomsman's gaze. "What do you need, sir?"

"I need you to escort Miss Warren to Lord Mountgarret's estate in Cardiff," Harry instructed, walking over to his desk. "If you depart now, you'll arrive before dark, but do not attempt to travel home this evening, wait until tomorrow to make the journey."

"Yes, sir," Jonathon confirmed, his eyes straying towards her.

Harry picked up the paper and extended it towards her. "When you arrive at Rumney Manor, go to the servant's entrance and ask for Mrs. Garvey. This note will explain everything."

"Thank you," she murmured, accepting the paper and tucking it into the pocket of her riding habit.

Turning his attention back to Jonathon, he said, "Go prepare your horse and Miss Warren's, but do not speak to anyone about this conversation."

Jonathon nodded and left the office, closing the door behind him.

Harry reached into the pocket of his jacket and pulled out a few coins. He extended them towards her. "This is all I have on me."

"I can't take your money," Emeline said, raising her hand to refuse him.

"You can, and you will," he insisted in a firm tone. "You need these coins more than I do at the moment."

Tentatively, she reached out and accepted them. "I'll pay you back once I can access my inheritance."

Harry smiled kindly at her. "I have no doubt." His smile dimmed as his eyes ran down the length of her. "We need to send you off with some clothing."

"I am confident that my lady's maid can secure a few dresses for me; discreetly, of course," Emeline said.

Harry nodded. "I fully believe that Priscilla has underestimated the staff's loyalty to you." He glanced out the window for a moment. "I'll contact your father's solicitor on your twenty-first birthday, and I will have him travel to speak to you at Lord Mountgarret's estate."

Feeling gratitude swell in her heart for her friend, she said, "Thank you for everything, Harry."

"Stay here until Jonathon is ready to depart," he ordered.

He placed his hand on the door handle. "I have no doubt that my sister will take good care of you. You need not fear for your safety."

"Thank you. That eases my mind."

A look of compassion filled his eyes. "I would accompany you myself, but I know that Mrs. Warren would notice my absence. However, I highly doubt she will notice if one of the younger groomsmen is missing."

"I understand."

"Your stepmother won't be able to hurt you in Cardiff," he assured her before he opened the door and departed.

Emeline stepped over to the window and watched as Harry headed towards the estate. She was immensely grateful for his assistance. She was well aware what was at stake if this plan failed. She had no doubt that her stepmother wouldn't hesitate to send her off to Bedlam.

Staying in Cardiff for the next two months wouldn't be so

bad, she thought. She might even be able to borrow some books from Lord Mountgarret's library. The good news was that she would be far away from her stepmother and stepsister.

With her riding hat in her hand, Emeline stood in front of Rumney Manor. She stared up at the three-level brick house with its slate roof and large bay windows.

"The servant's entrance will be around back, Miss Warren," Jonathon prodded from behind her as he held the horse's reins. A bag was slung over his shoulder.

Emeline turned towards the groomsman. "Thank you for accompanying me on my journey."

He tipped his head graciously. "You are welcome, miss. We rode hard and made good time."

"That we did. I just hope Mrs. Garvey will be as receptive as Harry indicated she would be."

"I have no doubt," Jonathon replied, urging the horses forward. "If you will excuse me, I need to go brush down these horses."

"Would you like me to come along? I can assist you."

Jonathon shook his head. "No, miss. You go on ahead to the servant's entrance, and I'll be along shortly."

Before she could reply, the door to the estate opened, revealing a tall man with an unusually large head and black hair.

"May I help you, miss?" he asked kindly.

She gave him a polite smile. "Thank you, sir. I am here to speak to Mrs. Garvey."

"Please, come in."

"Do not trouble yourself with me. I shall go around to the servant's entrance."

The man's brow lifted. "The servant's entrance is hardly the place for a lady." He stepped to the side. "If you will come in, I will send for Mrs. Garvey."

Emeline recognized that she was fighting a losing battle, so she tilted her head in acknowledgment. After she walked into the entry hall, the man introduced himself. "My name is Jerome Drake, and I am the butler for Rumney Manor."

Her eyes roamed the small, rectangular entry hall. It was simply decorated with black and white floor tiles and ivory-colored walls. Along one wall was an ornate, curved staircase leading to the next level.

"May I inform Mrs. Garvey of who is calling?"

She pressed her lips together. A name. Dare she give one? Instead, she said, "I would prefer not to."

His face remained expressionless as he replied, "If you will remain here, miss."

Emeline watched as he walked down the hall and disappeared into a side room. A painting hung on the wall of a dry moat filled with green shrubbery and a cobblestone foot path. She stepped closer and admired the brush-stroke of the artist.

A short time later, a woman, wearing a drab, brown, long-sleeved dress, approached her from the opposite side of the hall. Emeline had to smile, because the woman shared similar features to her dear friend Harry, including her faded brown hair and kind eyes.

"My name is Mrs. Garvey, and I'm the housekeeper," she said. "How may I help you?"

Reaching into the pocket of her riding habit, Emeline pulled out the missive and extended it towards her. "It would be best if you read your brother's note first."

Mrs. Garvey's face paled as she accepted the note. "Is he all right?"

"He is," she rushed to assure her.

Letting out a breath of relief, the housekeeper opened the note and began reading. Her frown seemed to intensify with every line that she read. When she finished, she folded the note and slipped it into the folds of her dress.

To her surprise, the housekeeper met her gaze and smiled. "This is most welcoming news."

"It is?"

"Follow me," Mrs. Garvey ordered. "We have much to discuss."

Emeline trailed closely behind as the housekeeper led her into the drawing room and closed the door.

Mrs. Garvey pointed towards the settee, indicating she should sit. "From this letter, I understand you are looking for a place to stay until your twenty-first birthday, which is in two months."

"That is correct," Emeline said as she sat down on a yellow camelback settee.

Mrs. Garvey nodded approvingly. "This could work."

"Thank you, Mrs. Garvey…" she started.

The housekeeper held up her hand. "Are you educated?"

"Yes. I attended Miss Bell's Finishing School in Bath."

"Which languages do you speak?"

"French, Italian, and German."

Mrs. Garvey walked further into the room. "How many instruments do you play?"

"Two. The pianoforte and harp."

"I assume you are proficient at needlework."

She nodded. "I am."

"Can you sing?"

"Yes."

Clasping her hands in front of her, Mrs. Garvey asked, "Have you had a Season yet?"

"I have had three."

The housekeeper gave her an astonished look. "May I ask why you are not married then? You are a beautiful young woman and come from the aristocracy. Do you have a defect that I need to be aware of?"

Emeline was unsure how to answer that question. She didn't think she was flawed in any way. "Not that I am aware of," she stated.

"My brother's letter indicated your stepmother intends to force you to marry an earl or commit you into a lunatic asylum."

"That is correct."

Taking a step closer to her, Mrs. Garvey asked, "Are you mad?"

"I assure you that I am not."

"Then I must pose the question," the housekeeper began, "why would you not wish to marry an earl?"

Tilting her chin to meet her curious gaze, Emeline responded, "I want to marry for love."

"I see, and you could not learn to love this earl?"

"I could not," she admitted. "He is as old as my father."

Mrs. Garvey bobbed her head. "I understand the problem, then."

Shifting in her seat, Emeline added, "After I reach my majority, I will be able to reimburse you for my room and board."

"That is the least of my concerns," Mrs. Garvey asserted. "Although, I do have a proposition for you."

"Which is?"

The housekeeper came to sit next to her on the settee. "Lord Mountgarret recently became the guardian of two young girls, who are arriving today. We've been searching for a woman of gentle birth, such as yourself, to fill the position of governess."

Emeline's mouth fell open, and she quickly snapped it shut. She swallowed the protest welling up within her. She could not be a governess. She had never even been around children. She finally found her voice.

"I am wholly unqualified to be a governess, Mrs. Garvey."

"I disagree. You are more than capable of filling the role. Besides, it would just be a temporary position, at least until someone responds to our ad in the newspapers," Mrs. Garvey said in a reassuring tone. "Furthermore, you would be doing me a great favor."

"I have never had a governess before," she admitted. "My mother educated me until I was sent off to boarding school."

"I have no doubt that you will rise to the task."

"How can you be so sure?"

"It's clear that my brother holds you in high regard."

"He is far too complementary of me." She smiled. "From my earliest memories, Harry has been involved in my life. He taught me how to ride, and he still escorts me whenever I go riding."

Mrs. Garvey turned her gaze out the window and was silent for a moment.

"These poor girls lost their parents in a horrible carriage accident," she finally said. "They are alone in the world, without any friends or family to speak of."

"How dreadful!"

"I believe these girls would benefit more from love and kindness at this time than a rigorous education schedule." Mrs. Garvey's face softened. "If I recall correctly from my brother's letters, you lost your own mother a few years ago."

Growing pensive, Emeline replied, "It's been five years and eight days."

"Will you not help these girls? They've suffered so much at such a young age," the housekeeper pleaded.

Emeline's heart broke for these two young girls. How could she not help them for the next two months as they sorted through their grief and heartache?

"I will stay on as their governess until my twenty-first birthday, or until you secure another governess."

Mrs. Garvey gave her a tentative smile. "The wages set for the governess are £24 per annum, and you will be provided with room and board."

"I am to room with the girls then?"

"It is customary for the governess to sleep in the nursery with her charges," Mrs. Garvey shared. "Is that not acceptable?"

Glancing down at her riding habit, she asked in a soft tone, "How will I dress myself?"

"I shall come in every morning and night to help you change."

"Thank you," she said in a relieved tone. "Although, I left my estate with only three dresses. I hope that will be sufficient."

Mrs. Garvey laughed. "My dear, most of the servants at Rumney House only have one dress to speak of."

"Will I be required to wear a uniform?"

"No," the housekeeper answered with a shake of her head. "Governesses are allowed to wear their own clothing."

Smoothing out her riding habit, she asked, "Are governesses allowed to go riding?"

"They are."

"Excellent. I brought my own horse with me."

An amused smile came to Mrs. Garvey's lips. "You brought your own horse?"

"I did," she replied. "I hope that is not a problem."

"It's not. Let's hope that Lord Mountgarret does not notice your horse in the stable. After all, governesses are generally in reduced circumstances, in need of earning their own living."

With a fleeting glance at the door, she lowered her voice. "Is Lord Mountgarret in residence?"

"We do not expect him until next week." Mrs. Garvey rose from the settee. "Perhaps it would be best if I show you to your room."

"How old are the girls?"

"Miss Phoebe is ten and Miss Sophia is eight."

Rising, Emeline sighed. "That's so young to lose one's parents."

"It is." Mrs. Garvey went and opened the door. "Did you ride alone to Rumney Manor?"

Emeline trailed behind Mrs. Garvey as she explained. "No, I was escorted by a groomsman from my estate. He went to tend to the horses when Mr. Drake invited me to come inside. I had intended to walk around to the servant's quarters."

"I am glad that you didn't," the housekeeper said as she started climbing the stairs. "A lady does not ever come in by the way of the servant's quarters."

Placing a hand on the banister, Emeline replied, "But I am incognito."

Mrs. Garvey laughed. "My dear, it is quite obvious that you are a lady. The quality of your riding habit alone gives you away."

"At my estate, I entered through the servant's quarters all the time to avoid my stepmother and stepsister," she revealed.

"Speaking of that," Mrs. Garvey said, glancing over her shoulder before continuing, "it might be best to change your name. Just as a precaution."

Emeline huffed. "I doubt my stepmother will send inquiries about me. She will be ecstatic to find that I am gone."

"True, but may I suggest we just shorten your name to Wren." Mrs. Garvey came to a stop at the top of the stairs. "It is close enough to your surname, but it is still slightly different."

"You want me to go by 'Miss Wren'?"

"Just for the time being," the housekeeper encouraged.

"If you think that's best."

"I do."

Mr. Drake appeared below them at the base of the stairs. "A coach has just pulled up. Miss Sophia and Miss Phoebe have arrived."

"It would appear we have to cut our tour short, Miss Wren," Mrs. Garvey said. "It's time for you to meet your charges."

4

EMELINE TRAILED BEHIND MRS. GARVEY AS THEY EXITED Rumney Manor. A footman had just opened the door of the coach and placed his hand out to assist the occupants.

A gloved hand slipped into his, and a stern-looking woman stepped out. She wore a tan-colored gown with a lacy collar, and her bun was fastened severely at the base of her neck.

Once her feet were on solid ground, the woman withdrew her hand and quickly approached them. "My name is Mrs. Reid," she stated in a haughty tone, "and I was hired to chaperone the children as far as Rumney Manor." She stepped closer and lowered her voice. "Good luck with those insolent brats. I will collect my pay and be on my way."

Emeline watched as two young children tentatively emerged from the coach. The girls were blonde-haired, fair-skinned, and both had round, innocent faces. Dressed in loose-fitting white shifts, the older sister kept a firm hand on the younger girl's shoulder as they remained by the coach.

"They don't look disobedient to me," Emeline commented.

Mrs. Reid scoffed. "Try traveling with them for days on end," she snapped. "They were rude, disrespectful, and refused to listen to even the simplest command. I daresay that they are past…"

Having heard enough of this woman's pompous attitude, Emeline cut the woman off. "Good day to you, Mrs. Reid."

"Well, I never," Mrs. Reid proclaimed as she turned her attention to Mrs. Garvey.

Emeline walked slowly towards the girls. She smiled as she crouched down to their level. "My name is Miss Wren. What are your names?"

The younger girl spoke up first. "My name is Sophia."

Turning her expectant gaze towards the older girl, Emeline was disappointed to see the girl staring daggers at her.

Sophia placed a hand to the side of her mouth and said, "That's Phoebe."

"Is Phoebe shy?" Emeline asked, mimicking Sophia's hand-to-her-mouth gesture.

"No," Sophia confirmed. "She's just angry."

Dropping her hand, Emeline replied, "I believe she has every right to be angry."

"You do?" Sophia asked, surprised.

"I do," she replied, lowering her voice. "I would be angry too, if I had to share a coach with Mrs. Reid." She grimaced.

Sophia laughed, and Phoebe's lips twitched. Well, that's a small victory, Emeline thought.

Rising from her crouched position, Emeline extended her hands to the two girls. Sophia immediately slipped her hand into hers, but Phoebe crossed her arms over her chest. Not deterred by her rejection, she lowered her hand.

"Will you take me on a tour of your new home?" Emeline asked as she led Sophia to the door.

Sophia looked up at her in surprise. "But I have never been here before."

"Neither have I. Believe it or not, I only just arrived thirty minutes before you," she confessed. "Perhaps we can take a tour of the estate together." She glanced over her shoulder to Phoebe and asked, "What do you say Miss Phoebe?"

Phoebe didn't respond and continued to glower at her.

"Will you please refrain from being such a chatterbox while we are on our tour, Phoebe," Emeline instructed in a mock stern tone.

Sophia laughed and placed her hand in front of her mouth. "You're silly."

"I'm not trying to be," Emeline said. "I suppose Phoebe just brings out the funny side of me."

"But she isn't saying anything," Sophia remarked.

"Isn't she?" she teased.

Mr. Drake was at the top of the stairs, holding open the door. Emeline stopped and provided the introductions.

"Girls, this is Mr. Drake. He's the butler of Rumney Manor." She cocked her head. "Do you have any interesting talents that we should know about, Mr. Drake?"

"I can play the guitar," he announced proudly.

"You can?" Sophia asked.

He nodded.

Sophia looked up at her with pleading eyes. "Can I learn how to play the guitar?"

"I don't see why not, assuming you also learn how to play the pianoforte."

A smile came to Sophia's face. "I already know how to play that instrument."

"That's great news," she praised. "I look forward to hearing you play tomorrow."

When they walked into the entry hall, Emeline put her hands up and announced, "Welcome to the entry hall!" She pointed towards the door on her right. "That's the drawing room."

Mrs. Garvey approached them with an amused expression on her face. "It might be best if I gave everyone a tour of the estate.

I daresay that Miss Wren's tour might be lacking in many regards."

"Well, I never," Emeline huffed in an imitation of Mrs. Reid. She winked at Sophia to let her know she was teasing. Phoebe followed behind, arms still crossed.

As they toured the first level, they visited Lord Mountgarret's study, a drawing room, the dining room, library, and a parlor. The second level housed the bedchambers and the nursery.

"The third level is where the household staff sleeps," Mrs. Garvey shared as she stopped outside of the nursery door. She pushed opened the door, revealing a common area and two rooms.

Sophia rushed in to look at the toys lining the walls, but Phoebe entered slowly, attempting to appear uninterested.

Keeping her voice low, she asked Mrs. Garvey, "Where did all these toys come from?"

"Lord Mountgarret."

"That was most thoughtful of him."

Mrs. Garvey smiled. "It was, wasn't it?"

The way she said it caused Emeline to pause. "You purchased them, didn't you?" she asked softly.

"I did, but I charged them to Lord Mountgarret's account."

She grinned as she saw Phoebe reach for a wooden Dutch doll. "You've made the girls very happy."

"I would hope so." Mrs. Garvey walked over to one of the doors. "This is your room, Miss Wren."

Emeline walked over and saw a room barely large enough to contain a bed. A small table sat next to it with a basin and pitcher on top.

"I imagine it's much smaller than you are accustomed to," Mrs. Garvey whispered.

"It is," Emeline admitted, "but it's only for two months."

"I find that you can do anything for two months."

Emeline smiled. "Well said, Mrs. Garvey. You sound a lot like your brother."

"I'm hoping that is a compliment."

"I assure you that it is," Emeline replied, turning her attention back to the girls.

With animated hands, Sophia was showing her sister the toy theatre in the corner, and she was smiling from ear to ear. Phoebe wasn't frowning anymore, but she wasn't exactly smiling either.

"This is the girls' room," Mrs. Garvey said, approaching the other door.

Peering inside, Emeline saw two beds and a wardrobe in the corner. "This room is much more spacious," she commented with a wry grin.

Mrs. Garvey clasped her hands together. "If there is nothing else, I will leave you with your two charges."

"I think that's a marvelous idea."

Mrs. Garvey nodded approvingly. "I shall send supper up shortly."

"Thank you," she replied.

Emeline watched as Mrs. Garvey departed the room before she clapped her hands together. "Girls! Come here, please."

Sophia and Phoebe put the toys down and cautiously approached her. So as to not appear too intimidating, Emeline reached for a stool and sat down.

"Now that we're finally alone, I thought we could get to know each other," she said.

Sophia and Phoebe both came to sit down in front of her, but they lowered their gazes to the floor.

"I shall go first," she announced. "I've never been a governess before. I was hoping you could give me some advice."

Phoebe looked up at her and asked, "Never?"

"Never," she repeated with a shake of her head.

A mischievous smile came to Phoebe's lips. "In that case,

you should know it is perfectly acceptable for us to engage in skipping ropes."

"Is that so?" Emeline questioned, attempting not to smile. She knew full well that skipping ropes was frowned on for girls. "I was under the impression it was unhealthy for girls to engage in such strenuous exercise."

"It is not," Phoebe said solemnly.

Turning her attention to the window, Emeline saw a large tree. "I had a friend at finishing school that used to love climbing trees. Would you like to do that one day?"

Phoebe's mouth dropped. "You would let us climb trees?"

"I would, assuming you followed very strict rules."

Sophia bobbed her head in an exaggerated fashion. "We would, wouldn't we, Phoebe?"

"Most definitely," Phoebe replied.

Leaning closer to the girls, Emeline asked, "May I ask what you did to Mrs. Reid to cause her to become so agitated earlier?"

With a guilty expression on her face, Phoebe lowered her gaze to the floor.

"Phoebe?" she prodded.

She brought her gaze back up. "Mrs. Reid kept chastising us for the smallest infractions, so I brought a frog into the coach with me."

"A frog?" Emeline's eyebrows shot up.

Phoebe nodded. "It was just a tiny, harmless frog."

Sophia giggled. "Mrs. Reid started squealing when the frog jumped onto her lap."

"I see," she stated, attempting to stifle her growing smile. "I don't blame you. Just try to keep frogs out of the estate… for now."

"Why was Mrs. Reid so mean to us?" Sophia asked innocently.

Emeline took a moment to consider her words.

"Sometimes people act a certain way because they're struggling in other aspects of their lives." She met Sophia's gaze. "But if you can, always choose kindness. Life is much easier that way."

"Mrs. Reid was not very kind," Phoebe said.

"No, she was not," Emeline agreed, "and how did that make you feel?"

"Sad," Sophia replied.

Phoebe frowned. "Mad."

"Exactly," she replied, "but kindness is infectious. Imagine how different your carriage ride would have been if Mrs. Reid had chosen kindness."

A knock came at the door before it was pushed open. A maid carrying a tray of food entered. "Here's your supper, miss," she stated as she placed it on the small, round table in the corner of the room.

"Thank you," Emeline replied, rising from the stool.

The maid curtsied. "Can I get you anything else?"

"What's your name?"

"Betty," she replied with a shy smile.

Emeline returned her smile graciously. "Well, Betty, thank you for bringing up our supper."

"You're most welcome," Betty answered, her smile widening.

"I propose we have supper and go to bed early tonight," Emeline suggested after the maid departed. "We've all traveled far today, and I, for one, am exhausted."

Sophia yawned. "Can you tell us a story while we eat?"

"I suppose I can tell you a story," she said, coming to sit at the table. "A long time ago, in a land far, far away, there lived a young woman named Emie. She had a wonderful childhood with doting parents, and she even had her own horse to ride whenever she wanted. She was blissfully happy."

The girls came to sit down at the table, both appearing to be enthralled by her story.

Emeline continued. "That was until her mother died. Then, her father decided that she needed a new mother and married a woman that appeared kind but was really mean."

"Like Mrs. Reid?" Sophia asked.

"Yes, exactly like her. I believe that Emie's stepmother and Mrs. Reid would be the best of friends," she joked.

"What happened next?" Phoebe asked.

"Well, Emie didn't get just a stepmother, but she also got a stepsister. Her stepsister was named Juliet, and even though she was beautiful, she was a half-wit."

Phoebe and Sophia started giggling.

"One day, while Emie's father was traveling on business, Emie overheard her stepmother and stepsister hatching a plot to hurt her. They planned to lock her in her bedchamber and never let her out. So, she ran out of her home and didn't stop running until she came upon a castle in the woods."

Emeline smiled at the excited looks on the girls' faces as she pressed on with her story. "Emie marched right up to the main door and asked to speak to the master of the house."

"She did?" Sophia asked.

She nodded. "She did."

"What did he say?" Phoebe asked as she picked up a piece of bread off her plate.

"Well, it turns out the handsome lord was looking for a governess for his two girls."

"He was?" Sophia asked with wide eyes.

"He was," she confirmed.

"What were the girls' names?" Phoebe inquired.

She pretended to mull over her question for a moment.

"Their names were Phoebe and Sophia."

Both girls smiled, clearly amused by her choice of names.

Emeline turned her attention towards their plates of food. "I will finish the story later. But, for now, you need to eat your supper."

The girls nodded obediently as they started eating. As she watched them, Emeline realized that being a governess didn't seem to be so hard. She would just befriend the children and love them. Because everyone deserved to be loved.

Emeline woke up, startled. Someone was crying. She sat up on her small bed and brought her hand to her forehead. Suddenly, everything came back to her, and she remembered that she was a governess. One of the girls must be crying, she thought, as she threw off her covers.

She took the time to light a candle before she hurried across the common area to the girls' room. Sophia was crying and moaning the word "Mother".

A quick glance over at Phoebe's bed, and she saw the girl was sitting up in bed with a sad expression on her face.

"It's been this way since Mother and Father died," Phoebe admitted, her voice hitching.

Emeline nodded her understanding as she put the candle down on the table. Crouching down next to Sophia, she whispered, "It will be all right, little one."

Her voice seemed to calm Sophia, but the tears were still forming in her eyes. She rose, sat down on the bed, and reached over to cradle Sophia in her arms. Gently, she rocked the girl back and forth as she murmured, "You're going to be just fine."

After a short time, Sophia's breathing deepened. She had fallen back to sleep.

Phoebe spoke up from her side of the room. "Sophia would never calm down for me. Sometimes her crying went on for hours."

"My mother died five years ago," Emeline found herself admitting. "After she died, everyone was supportive and kind during the day, but it was different at night. I was alone in my bed, and I just wanted to be wrapped up in my mother's embrace."

Tears came to Phoebe's eyes. "I miss my mother and father so much that it hurts."

"As well you should. You loved your parents with your whole heart," Emeline replied. "Everything you are feeling is normal."

Phoebe lowered her gaze towards her bed. "I feel anger. I find that I am mad all the time."

Kissing the top of Sophia's head, she replied, "Anger is normal, as well. I'll bet you feel mad that you were cheated out of time with your parents."

"I do. It isn't fair."

"Life isn't fair." Emeline leaned her back against the wall. "Some people are given impossible challenges to overcome, whereas others appear to have a life of ease."

Phoebe tucked her knees under her chin. "I wish I had a life of ease."

Emeline shook her head. "There's no such thing. It just appears that way. Everyone has challenges and obstacles in this life. Some are just more visible than others."

"I just want my mother and father back," Phoebe cried.

"I know, but it will be all right," she murmured reassuringly.

Phoebe huffed. "How? How will it be all right without my mother and father around?"

"You'll find ways to adjust, and life will become easier over time." She hesitated before adding, "My mother taught me an abundance of things in my life, except how to get through life without *her*."

Phoebe's voice shook as she admitted, "I'm scared."

"What are you scared of?"

"Living life without my parents," was her simple reply.

Emeline listened to Sophia let out a slight snore, and a smile came to her face. "No one can prepare you for losing a loved one, but it does get easier. Every day, you become stronger and stronger, but you will never forget your mother and father. They are imprinted on your very soul."

Tears rolled down Phoebe's face. "Sophia and I are all alone in this world."

"No, you are not alone," Emeline rushed to assure her. "For starters, you have me."

"You are *just* the governess."

She smiled. "I would rather title myself as a governess extraordinaire."

Her words brought a smile to the girl's lips, but it quickly disappeared with her next question. "Why does Lord Mountgarret not like us?"

"Why would you say that?"

Phoebe frowned. "He hired Mrs. Reid to escort us from our country estate to Rumney Manor."

"I admit that Mrs. Reid was rather a poor choice…"

The girl interjected, "And I heard Mrs. Reid telling our housekeeper that Lord Mountgarret didn't even want us to come to Rumney Manor." She lowered her voice as her eyes darted to Sophia. "She said he didn't want us at all."

"That's utter nonsense. I wouldn't believe anything that comes out of Mrs. Reid's mouth," Emeline stated firmly, hoping her words were true.

Phoebe pulled her covers over her knees. "Then why wasn't he here to greet us?"

"That, I cannot say," she reluctantly admitted.

"He hates us," Phoebe said, her shoulders slumping.

"No, no, no…" Emeline argued. "That's not true. Look at all the toys that he had waiting for you."

Phoebe didn't appear convinced, so she continued, "Furthermore, Lord Mountgarret is an important man, and he most likely had a good reason why he couldn't be here for your arrival."

"But the Season is over."

"True, but he probably had business he had to attend to in London."

Her answer appeared to appease Phoebe, and the girl didn't look as troubled. "I hadn't thought of that."

"He'll be here soon enough, and until then, we shall have such fun."

"Fun?" Phoebe asked with an uplifted brow. "Governesses aren't supposed to be fun."

A playful smile came to her lips. "After breakfast, we shall have a wide assortment of lessons, including the study of French, needlework, and botany. The afternoon is dedicated to music, and the evening will be filled with rational amusement and instructive conversation."

Phoebe scrunched her nose. "That doesn't sound like fun."

"Oh, my dear girl, you have never had a lesson prepared by me," Emeline replied, her tone smug.

A yawn escaped Phoebe's lips. "I suppose not."

"Go back to bed," Emeline encouraged. She was pleased when she saw Phoebe lay her head down on her pillow.

As she started to move off the bed, Sophia protested and whined, "Don't go."

Emeline didn't have the heart to leave Sophia just yet, so she leaned over and blew out the candle. She would just remain here a little longer, and then she would slip out of the room undetected. She snuggled Sophia a bit closer and rested the back of her head against the wall.

Within a few moments, she and the girls had fallen fast asleep.

5

Baldwin adjusted the stack of ledgers next to him in the coach. He had an exorbitant amount of work that he should be doing for Foster Company. Instead, he was traveling to Rumney Manor to check on his two wards.

It had been more than a week since they'd arrived at his estate. He was curious how they were adjusting and whether his housekeeper had been able to hire a governess. Once he confirmed they were settled, he had every intention of returning to London.

Without them.

The coach came to a stop outside of his estate. He put his hand through the window and opened the door, not bothering to wait for the footman to assist him. Reaching back, he gathered the ledgers into his arms and walked towards the main entrance.

The door opened, and Mr. Drake extended his hands to collect the books. "Allow me, milord."

"I have them," Baldwin said, shifting them in his arms. "Will you show Mr. Barnet to my office when he arrives?"

"As you wish."

Baldwin took a step towards his study tucked away in the

rear of his estate, but then he spun back around. "Was Mrs. Garvey able to hire a governess?"

"She was," Mr. Drake confirmed.

"Do you find her suitable?"

"I find Miss Wren to be more than suitable, milord."

"Excellent. Will you inform the governess I wish to speak to her?"

Mr. Drake's eyes shifted towards the window. "I will, but I just saw Miss Wren and the girls leaving for their morning walk."

He frowned. "Mornings are reserved for lessons, not frivolous outings."

"If I may," the butler started, "Miss Wren is quite effective with the girls."

"I shall determine that for myself," Baldwin replied as he turned to walk down the hall.

Baldwin didn't stop until he came around his desk and set the ledgers down. He sat in his chair and reached for the top ledger. It was some time later when he heard a quiet knock at the door.

"Morning, Lord Mountgarret," a familiar voice greeted.

He looked up from his books and saw his friend and man of business, Henry Barnet. He rose from his chair. "Good morning, Henry. Thank you for agreeing to see me so early."

"It's my privilege. Besides, I haven't seen you in nearly six months."

Baldwin returned to his chair. "Running Foster Company has been much more demanding than I anticipated."

Walking further into the room, his friend held two books in his hand. "I'm truly happy for you. You've worked hard, and you've accomplished many great things."

"It had little to do with hard work and more to do with good fortune," Baldwin declared. "The Duke of Blackbourne paid off my outstanding debts, then paid for Rumney Manor to be repaired. Furthermore, Penelope graciously offered me the opportunity to be a part owner with her at Foster Company."

"Regardless, you have taken what you were given and increased it many times over."

Baldwin closed the ledger in front of him and pushed it to the side. "That's true. My father left me in financial ruins, and I intend never to make his mistakes."

"That won't be too hard," Henry muttered. "Your father was a scoundrel."

"That he was."

Coming to sit down in front of the desk, Henry placed the books on the table. "If your father hadn't died, I have no doubt he would have been thrown into debtor's prison. He repeatedly took out loans to pay for his gambling habit."

"Don't forget he had to support his mistresses, as well," Baldwin added bitterly.

Henry huffed. "How can we forget that? Your father was so callous as to flaunt them in front of your mother."

"My poor mother. She endured so much from him."

"That she did." His friend grew pensive. "But she would be proud of you and all that you have overcome."

Baldwin nodded in agreement. "She would, especially since Penelope and I have been reunited."

Opening one of the books, Henry shared, "I bring more good news. Last year at this time, your estate was producing £75 per year, but now, with all the updated equipment you bought for the farmers, I project it will produce £550 this year."

"That's fantastic news!" he exclaimed as he reached for the book.

"I thought you'd be pleased. Although, I'm sure that's a paltry sum compared to your income at Foster Company."

"It is. However, I am grateful for any sort of income." Baldwin reviewed the book for a moment. "Take the profit and buy more land."

"I assumed you'd request that, so I've already made some inquiries."

"Excellent. We can expand the farmland."

A child's laughter came drifting through the window, and Henry shot him a questioning look. "Is that a child laughing?"

He frowned, his mood now turning sour. "It is."

"Is it yours?" his friend asked in a low, hesitant voice.

Baldwin's mouth dropped open. "Heavens, no!" he declared forcefully. "Thomas Barrington and his wife died in a carriage accident, and he listed *me* as the guardian to his two girls."

"I am sorry for your loss," Henry murmured.

"Thank you. It was most unexpected." His eyes drifted towards the window as he heard another fit of laughter. They had tarried outside long enough. The girls should be in the nursery working on their lessons.

"What are their ages?"

"One is ten, and the other is eight."

Henry started laughing, clearly amused by his misfortune.

"It's not funny," Baldwin protested.

"Isn't it, though?" Henry stated.

"No."

"Just a little?"

He shook his head. "It is not even remotely amusing."

With a broad smile on his face, his friend asked, "What are you going to do with two girls underfoot?"

"Mrs. Garvey hired a governess to rear the girls."

"I see," Henry said. "Is that the end of your contribution?"

"What more can I do?" he asked with a puzzled expression.

Henry's smile vanished. "You're serious?"

"I am."

"You intend to let a governess raise these two girls."

Baldwin nodded. "At least until I can send them off to boarding school."

Henry shot him a look of disbelief. "Didn't your father treat you the same way?"

"That's different," he declared. "It's perfectly acceptable to be sent off to Eton College at thirteen years old."

"True, but prior to that, he rarely spent time with you," Henry pressed.

"My mother filled that void."

Henry rose from his chair. "But they don't have a mother. *You* are all they have now."

"They are not my children," Baldwin asserted. "Truth be told, I never even wanted children."

Reaching down, Henry picked up the books he brought with him from the desk. "You don't have a choice now. You are the guardian to two girls who need you."

"I disagree. Why would they need me? I am a perfect stranger to them."

Henry stepped over to the window and looked out over the green fields. "Your governess is a pretty thing."

He stiffened. "I don't dally with the help."

"I know," Henry said, glancing his way. "You aren't your father."

Rising, Baldwin walked over to the window. He saw the two girls laughing as they were running around in the field. A brown-haired young woman, wearing a fashionable white gown, was giving them some sort of instructions. Small curls ran along her forehead, and large curls framed her oval face. She was remarkably beautiful.

"What do you think they're doing?" his friend asked.

Huffing, he replied, "They appear to be squandering away their time. They should be up in the nursery working on French or practicing their needlework."

"Children need time to play."

"I disagree. Children need discipline."

Turning his expectant gaze towards Baldwin, Henry inquired, "If that will be all?"

Baldwin nodded. "Please notify me at once if the inquiries pan out."

"As you wish," Henry said.

Baldwin continued to stare out the window as Henry departed. He needed to have a serious talk with Miss Wren about the children and their studies. They had too much to learn to just waste the day away in frivolous activities.

Miss Wren waved the girls closer and pointed towards the woodlands lining the back of his estate. They started walking swiftly towards the dense cluster of trees. He wanted to bang on the glass to alert her of the dangers lurking inside those woods. There were snakes, bats, and other creatures in those woods.

Foolish woman, he thought, as he rushed out of his study and headed towards the main door.

By the time he stepped outside of the manor and rounded the corner, they had vanished into the trees. He hurried towards the spot where he'd last seen them and entered into the peaceful serenity of the woods.

The sights and sounds filled his senses as he ventured further. He heard woodpeckers drumming in the trees in the distance. Bluebells lined the moist floor as he walked cautiously further into the trees, being mindful of where he placed his feet. He didn't want to disturb any snakes.

Up ahead, he saw a rushing stream where he'd spent his youth playing. Before he took another step, he heard a child's laughter. He crouched low and attempted to keep himself hidden from view. He wanted to see what they were up to. After a moment, he ducked behind a tree and watched as the older girl dipped her hands into the stream. It took him a moment to remember the older girl's name was Phoebe.

She pulled her hand out of the water and announced, "I got one."

"Is it big?" the governess asked.

She nodded as she turned to show Miss Wren. "Bigger than the last one."

"Let me see."

Phoebe lifted a large bullfrog up, holding onto it tightly so it wouldn't escape. Its tongue flicked out twice, then it croaked.

"My, that *is* big," the governess admitted. "Show your sister."

The younger one put her hands out, and her sister put it into her hands. "This one is slimy," she said.

"It is," Phoebe replied.

Miss Wren gasped as her attention became focused on a bush near the stream. "Sophia, put down the frog and come look at this. I found mint plants."

The girls came to stand next to the governess as she explained, "A mint plant has long branches that grow upward and then hang down. The plant has spikes or white or pinkish flowers and rough, fuzzy, jagged leaves."

Miss Wren picked off three leaves and extended one to each of the girls. "Try it."

The girls obediently ate the leaves as Miss Wren placed one on the top of her tongue.

"Mint is marvelous for calming the stomach, good for watery eyes, cures mouth sores, and prevents ill-smelling breath," Miss Wren listed.

Phoebe smiled as she plucked another leaf off the plant. "It also tastes delicious."

The governess rose and asked, "What other plants can we find in these woods?"

The younger girl spoke up. "Chamomile?"

"Good, Sophia," Miss Wren praised. "Chamomile is indigenous to England. What is it used for?"

Phoebe answered, "It helps with indigestion and gas."

"Well done, girls," Miss Wren said. "You are both quite knowledgeable about botany."

Feeling slightly foolish for eavesdropping, Baldwin decided he'd heard enough. It was evident that she was teaching the girls their lessons in an unconventional way, yet it appeared to be working.

He took a step back and inadvertently snapped a twig.

In response, Miss Wren quickly corralled the children behind her and demanded, "Who's there?"

"Blazes," he muttered under his breath. Now he had to make his presence known.

The moment the twig snapped, Emeline knew that they were not alone. But who could be spying on them? And for what purpose?

Keeping the children tucked safely behind her, she scanned the trees, half hoping to see a large animal hopping away. She was not so lucky. A man dressed in a grey jacket, white waistcoat, dark trousers, and a white cravat stepped out from behind a tree. He was tall and thin-framed, with a narrow nose. His dark brown hair was brushed forward.

Ignoring the fact that this man was rather handsome, Emeline eyed a large stick lying near her feet. She was unsure of the risk that this man posed, and she was prepared to defend the girls.

He took a few steps closer to her and stopped. His stern expression relaxed into the suggestion of a smile.

"Morning," he called out.

She kept her gaze firmly fixed on him, but her tone was wary. "Morning."

"May I ask what you're doing in these woods, miss?"

Tilting her chin, she declared, "That is none of your concern, sir."

"Indeed, it is my concern, since it's my land you're trespassing on," he responded smugly.

Realization dawned. She recognized who this man was.

"You're Lord Mountgarret."

"I am."

Bringing the girls around to stand next to her, she provided the introductions. "Lord Mountgarret, allow me to introduce you to your wards, Miss Phoebe and Miss Sophia."

He bowed. "Girls."

The girls curtsied, but neither returned a greeting. They both kept their gaze downcast.

"I saw you running into the cover of the trees, and I came to inform you that this area isn't generally safe for women of gentle birth," he said, his eyes roaming the trees.

Emeline forced a smile to her lips. "That's most kind of you, my lord. However, I grew up near woodlands, and I assure you that I am aware of the risks."

"Be that as it may, I would prefer my wards to stay out of the woodlands," he pressed.

Pointing to the mint bush, she went on to explain, "We were having a lesson in botany today, and I was educating them about the different plants growing in these woodlands."

"Is there not a book on botany in my library?"

"There are many," she replied, "but I thought it would be best if I allowed them to see the plants in person."

His face grew solemn as he surveyed his wards. "Being outside without a bonnet is not good for a lady's complexion."

Glancing up at the tree canopy, Emeline contended, "But we're shaded under the trees."

"But there was no shade when they were running through the fields earlier," he pointed out.

"I see your point, my lord," she conceded, hoping to appease this nit-picky man.

Tugging down on the lapels of his jacket, he asserted, "I would prefer you to teach their lessons in the nursery."

The girls' panicked eyes sought hers out, and she responded by placing a hand on each one of their shoulders.

"I have found that the girls respond to more unconventional types of lessons. Perhaps we could discuss this further in private?" she asked.

Annoyance flashed on his features. "Return the children to the nursery and report to me in my study, Miss Wren. I fear we have much to discuss."

"As you wish," she murmured as she encouraged the girls forward.

Lord Mountgarret waited for them to pass by before he proceeded back to the estate. None of them spoke as they walked. Once they arrived, the girls swiftly headed up the stairs and down the hall to the nursery.

Emeline followed closely behind into the nursery, closing the door behind them.

Sophia spoke first. "Why does Lord Mountgarret not want us to be outside?"

"Don't worry. I'll speak to him and explain why it's so important for you to be outside," she assured the little girl.

Phoebe crossed her arms over her chest. "He doesn't care about us."

"That is not true," Emeline defended. "He was worried that you might get hurt in the woods."

Turning her head towards the window, Phoebe just let out a disbelieving huff.

"Practice your French until I get back." Emeline stepped over to the door and placed her hand on the handle. "Don't fret. I'm sure that Lord Mountgarret can be reasoned with," she said, hoping her words were true.

As she walked towards Lord Mountgarret's study, she

attempted to garner strength to speak to the infuriating man. The door to his study was open, and she knocked gently on the frame.

"Come in," he said, not bothering to look up from his desk.

She walked further into the room and waited for him to acknowledge her.

He rose and pointed towards the chair in front of the desk. "Please have a seat, Miss Wren."

"Thank you," she murmured as she sat down gracefully.

Lord Mountgarret clasped his hands behind his back and walked over to the window. "I am rather shocked and disappointed by your disrespectful behavior in front of the children."

"Pardon?"

She had not expected that.

"You seem to think it's appropriate to undermine me," he pressed.

She shook her head. "I assure you that was not my intention."

"Then what was your intention, Miss Wren?" he asked, pointedly looking back at her.

Attempting to reason with the man, she said, "I have discovered that the girls respond best when they are able to get some of their excessive energy out. That's why we take frequent walks."

"May I ask what your lesson schedule is like?"

"In the morning, we generally read, commence with our French and Italian lessons, sketch various objects, and I teach them about botany. After a midday meal, we adjourn to the music room where they practice the pianoforte, guitar, and singing."

"Guitar?"

She nodded. "It's becoming increasingly common for women to play the guitar."

"No guitar. I would prefer my wards to be taught the pianoforte and harp."

"But, my lord…"

He cut her off. "I have made my decision."

"Of course, but I think that's a mistake."

Lord Mountgarret arched an eyebrow. "I am not paying you for your opinions, Miss Wren. I am paying you to educate the girls."

"Then you are, in fact, paying for my opinions," she countered, squaring her shoulders. "I am teaching these girls everything required to be a proper lady."

He scoffed. "Except decorum."

Biting her sharp tongue, she continued. "In the evening, we retire to the nursery to practice our embroidery, and I allow Sophia to play before bed."

"Why would a girl of Sophia's age need to play before bed?"

"Because she's only eight."

He unclasped his hands. "Sophia should find enjoyment in embroidery."

"No eight-year-old finds enjoyment in embroidery, my lord," Emeline countered.

"Then reading, perhaps?"

Emeline clasped her hands in her lap. "I assure you that the girls read plenty throughout the day."

"Miss Wren, you seem to be confused by the hierarchy in this household," Lord Mountgarret stated. "When I make a decision, it is final. Understood?" He turned back to look out the window.

Pressing her lips together in a tight line, Emeline attempted to keep herself from answering. She knew if she spoke her mind, she would be fired. But she found she couldn't sit back and listen to this infuriating lord make poor decisions when it came to the girls.

"No," she replied softly.

"I beg your pardon?" he asked, turning to look at her with disbelief in his eyes.

Rising from her chair, she declared, "You may be their guardian, but you don't know these girls like I do."

"That may be true…"

She spoke over him, her words growing more determined. "I am not finished, Lord Mountgarret."

Lifting his brows in surprise, he closed his mouth.

"You weren't even here to greet them," she chided. "You sent a vile woman to accompany them who criticized them the entire way."

"Mrs. Reid came highly recommended," he argued.

"You sent a stranger to escort your wards. Why didn't you escort them yourself?"

"I was busy in London with…"

Interjecting, Emeline pleaded, "Sophia and Phoebe are good girls. They just want someone to love them, to care for them, but you have cast them aside. I beg of you, allow them to be children. Let them play outside, climb trees…"

"Climb trees?"

"Yes, climb trees. Let them go into the woodlands and explore."

Lord Mountgarret frowned. "Are you quite finished, Miss Wren?"

"No. I'm not." She tilted her chin. "Phoebe and Sophia just lost their parents. They need you to be present in their lives. You are the only father figure they have."

His frown intensified. "I am not their father," he growled. "I don't know how to raise girls."

She took a step towards him, her tone softening. "Then, let me help you."

"No," he said with a shake of his head. "You are fired."

She reared back. "Fired?"

"I cannot have a woman such as yourself teaching the girls."

"Such as myself?" she asked with a lifted brow.

Lord Mountgarret looked at her as though she were a simpleton. "You clearly lack decorum, and the good breeding necessary to govern my wards." He stepped over to his desk and pulled out a drawer. He retrieved two pounds and placed them on the desk. "Here are your earned wages and then some. You may take them and go."

"May I at least say goodbye to the children?" she asked as she approached the desk and collected the coins.

"You may," he replied.

Clutching the coins in her hands, she implored, "Please shower love and attention on Phoebe and Sophia. They need you…"

He interjected, "They are no longer your concern, Miss Wren. Kindly go and say your goodbyes before I change my mind."

Slowly, she backed out of the room. A grim-faced Mr. Drake stood at the bottom of the stairs.

"Goodbye, Mr. Drake," she said, stepping closer to him. "It was an honor getting to know you this past week."

"Likewise, Miss Wren."

Tears came to her eyes as she expressed, "I suppose I have to break the bad news to the girls."

"I don't know what they're going to do without you," Mr. Drake said, shaking his head slowly.

Glancing over her shoulder at the study, Emeline whispered, "I'll be staying at Mrs. Garvey's cottage if anyone needs me."

He gave her a kind smile in response.

She placed her hand on the banister as she walked slowly up the stairs. How was she going to break the news to them? They'd already been through so much.

Stopping outside of the nursery door, Emeline swiped at the tears streaming down her cheeks. She needed to be brave for the girls. Why had she not curbed her tongue, she wondered.

As she opened the door, Phoebe turned her head and her face blanched.

She knew.

"No, you can't leave!" she shouted, jumping up from her

chair. She ran into her waiting arms. "Please don't let him send you away."

Crouching down, Emeline placed her hands on Phoebe's shoulders. "I'll be staying at Mrs. Garvey's cottage for the next two months. I'll arrange for a time for us to meet. I promise."

Sophia came and threw her arms around her. "Please don't leave us."

A sob escaped Emeline's lips. "I have to. But Lord Mountgarret will find a governess that will love you just as much."

"You're lying," Phoebe said, tears rolling down her cheeks. "He hates us and wants us to be miserable."

"That's not true, I promise," Emeline argued.

Phoebe stomped her foot. "It *is* true. I hate him!"

Pulling her into a tight embrace, Emeline said, "It is not good to hate anyone. He's doing the best he knows how."

"By taking you away from us?" Phoebe asked in disbelief.

Emeline wiped the tears on Phoebe's cheeks. "Be patient with him. This is new to him as well."

A deep clearing of a throat came from the doorway. Lord Mountgarret's imposing figure filled the doorway as he said, "It would be best if you go now, Miss Wren."

Turning back towards the girls, she placed her hand on Sophia's cheek. "I won't be far. This is not goodbye."

Rising, she pulled them both in for another tight embrace. "I love you, girls."

Tears came to her eyes as she turned and left the room, brushing past Lord Mountgarret. Her heart shattered even more when she heard Sophia and Phoebe start sobbing.

Even though she had only been their governess for a little over a week, she had grown to love them rather quickly. They were so easy to love. Now she had to inform Mrs. Garvey of the bad news. She had no doubt that the housekeeper would let her stay in the cottage with her. However, she would find a way to see the girls again. This could not be a goodbye!

6

HOLDING A DRINK IN HIS HAND, BALDWIN SAT IN HIS STUDY, alone. Just as he preferred it. He kept replaying Miss Wren's words when she'd said her final goodbyes to the girls. She seemed so genuine in her affection, but how was that possible? She'd only known Phoebe and Sophia for a bit more than a week. Furthermore, her words of 'be patient with him' resonated deep within his soul. He had just fired her, but rather than complain or criticize him, she sympathized with him.

He brought the glass up to his lips. Regardless, it was the right decision to fire her, he told himself. She was impertinent and did not possess the calm demeanor necessary to raise Phoebe and Sophia. Miss Wren may have compassion, but that trait was not required for a governess. They were to be strict disciplinarians and ensure their charges are brought up to be well-accomplished young ladies.

No matter how hard he tried to convince himself that he'd been right, he still found himself doubting the decision. Why was that? As a businessman, he hired and fired people on a regular basis. And he'd never questioned his decisions... until now.

He placed his drink on the table next to the settee and rose, turning his attention to the darkened window. Even the staff did not seem pleased by his firing Miss Wren. Mrs. Garvey frowned disapprovingly when he'd informed her of his decision and promptly shared that it could take months to hire a new governess.

To make matters worse, after Miss Wren left the nursery, Phoebe and Sophia started sobbing uncontrollably and refused to leave the room. Mrs. Garvey had sent maids up to tend to them, but it did little to appease their melancholy.

He blew out the candle before he headed for his bedchamber on the second level. He'd just reached his bedchamber when he heard muffled sobbing coming from down the hall. He hung his head, feeling slightly guilty. The girls were still crying over Miss Wren. Poor things. However, if the girls didn't stop crying, then they might wake the whole household, and that was unacceptable.

Baldwin approached the nursery and opened the door. He walked swiftly to the girls' room and saw Sophia moaning in her bed, thrashing about. Phoebe was standing next to the bed trying to wake her sister up by shaking her shoulder.

"What is going on here?" he demanded.

Phoebe turned her head to acknowledge him. "She is having a bad dream."

"Can you wake her up?"

She shook her head. "No."

"How do you normally calm her down?"

"Miss Wren would speak to her in soothing tones, then cradle her in her arms."

Stepping closer to the bed, he stated, "Miss Wren isn't here. What can I do?"

Phoebe shrugged. "I don't know."

Baldwin placed a hand on her shoulder. He shook her gently. "Wake up, Sophia."

In response, Sophia cried out, "I want my mother!"

He shook her again, and in a louder voice, ordered, "Wake up." He waited a few moments before he tried again. "You need to wake up, Sophia."

The little girl just rolled over in bed, her heartfelt moans growing louder.

"How long has she been prone to bad dreams?" he asked.

"Since my parents died."

Glancing over at Phoebe, he questioned, "How long do these episodes last?"

"Sometimes for hours."

He groaned. What was he going to do? He didn't have any experience with bad dreams, or children for that matter. Furthermore, he didn't want Sophia's cries to wake the whole household.

"Can you go get Miss Wren... *please*?" Phoebe asked.

He winced as he admitted, "Unfortunately, I cannot. I don't even know where she is."

Phoebe's voice grew more confident as she shared, "Miss Wren is staying at Mrs. Garvey's cottage."

"She is?"

She nodded.

That was most fortunate news! He would go get Miss Wren to tend to Sophia. "I shall be right back."

He rushed out of the room, down the stairs, and out the main door. He didn't stop until he arrived at the small cottage near the stables. He banged on the door.

After what felt like hours, but was most likely only mere moments, the door opened, revealing Mrs. Garvey. She held a candle in her hand.

"What's wrong, Lord Mountgarret?" the housekeeper asked.

"It's Sophia," he spoke in a rush.

A gasp came from behind Mrs. Garvey, and Miss Wren came into view. She was wearing a white wrapper, and her brown hair was tied back into a low bun. "What's wrong with Sophia?" she questioned.

"She is having a bad dream, and I can't seem to calm her down."

Miss Wren's eyes grew determined. "Let me put on my boots."

A few moments later, Miss Wren exited the cottage and walked swiftly towards the estate. He easily caught up to her and matched her purposeful stride, but she didn't attempt to make conversation with him as they headed towards Rumney Manor.

As they walked down the hall towards the nursery, the sounds of Sophia's moaning seemed to intensify, echoing throughout the second level.

Phoebe let out a relieved sigh when they walked through the door. "You came."

"Of course, I came," Miss Wren said with a smile as she walked over to Sophia's bed and crouched down next to it. She placed her hand on Sophia's forehead and whispered reassuringly, "I'm here. You're safe, little one."

Her words had almost an immediate effect, and Sophia calmed down. Miss Wren then moved to sit on the bed and cradled Sophia in her arms.

Silence has never been so blissful, he mused, as he watched Miss Wren kiss Sophia tenderly on the head.

Miss Wren turned her attention towards Phoebe. "I have Sophia now. Why don't you get some sleep, dear?"

Phoebe nodded obediently and laid down in her bed. "Thank you for coming, Miss Wren."

"Always," she replied.

Baldwin stood back, unsure of what he should be doing. He felt like the encroacher in his own home.

"I shall take care of the girls tonight, Lord Mountgarret," Miss Wren said. "You may go off to bed."

"Thank you," he responded.

Lowering her gaze to the bed, it was evident that she was hoping he would leave, but he found himself lingering. He was curious how she could calm Sophia so effectively.

"How were you able to do that?" he asked, taking a step closer.

Miss Wren brought her gaze back up to his. "Sophia misses her mother. She just needs to feel loved and comforted."

"But you were able to calm her with just a few words."

"I suppose she could hear the heartache in my voice. We both lost our mothers at a young age," she replied wistfully.

He moved to sit down on the opposite edge of Sophia's bed. "When did you lose your mother?"

"Shortly before my sixteenth birthday."

"May I ask how she died?"

Shifting Sophia in her arms, Emeline shared, "She complained of stomach pain, mostly on her right side, and it kept getting worse. She collapsed one evening and died shortly thereafter."

"I am sorry for your loss," he said softly. "My mother died unexpectedly, as well. One day, she just didn't wake up."

"My condolences." She stared into his eyes for several moments as if to convey her sincerity.

"I visit her grave nearly every day that I'm at Rumney Manor." He averted his gaze towards the floor. Why did he feel the need to share that piece of information?

"I think that is commendable."

"You do?"

"I do," she replied. "To lose someone you love alters your life forever, but losing your mother is inexpressible." She grew quiet for a moment before adding, "Sometimes we must take a moment to remember what we lost, to find the strength to press forward."

He shifted on the bed until he could lean his back against the wall. "I miss my mother every day."

"As do I. Which is why I can sympathize with Phoebe and Sophia. In a blink of an eye, they lost both their mother and father."

His eyes darted over to a sleeping Phoebe, and he found himself admitting, "I don't know how to help these girls."

"Just show them kindness," Miss Wren answered.

A smile came to his lips. "My mother used to say something similar. She would always tell me to 'choose kindness'."

"That sounds like wise advice."

"It was."

Miss Wren surprised him by saying, "I am sorry for being so rude in your study earlier. I had no right to speak to you in such a manner."

"I understand why you did, and I think it's admirable how much you care for these girls."

"It's easy to care for them," she replied as a yawn escaped her lips. Her hand flew up to cover her mouth.

"I should go." He rose from the bed. "Thank you for coming to help Sophia, even after everything…" His voice trailed off.

She gave him a weak smile. "You don't need to explain yourself, my lord. Just be aware that I don't mind helping out with the girls."

"I believe I may have misjudged you, Miss Wren."

Her smile grew. "No, I don't believe you did. I *am* rather outspoken. It's just one of my many faults."

He found himself returning her smile before he turned to depart. Tomorrow, he would attempt to hire Miss Wren back as governess, but only on his terms. He would dictate exactly what was expected of her, and if she refused, then he would seek to hire another governess.

But she would agree to his terms. What choice did she have? She was an impoverished gentlewoman forced to work for an income.

Emeline picked up a book from the pile on the table. On her way out of Rumney Manor early that morning, she had stopped by the library and borrowed a handful of books. She'd been amazed by the selection of books that Lord Mountgarret had in his library. It had put the library at Cairnwood Hall to shame.

She stepped over to the chair by the hearth and opened to the first page of *Robinson Crusoe*. She'd already read this story, but it was one of her favorites.

A knock came at the door.

Rising, she placed the book down on the table. She took a moment to smooth out her pale-yellow gown. She glanced down to be sure that its square neckline was straight before she answered the door. To her surprise, Lord Mountgarret stood outside with his top hat in his right hand. She assumed the worst and flung the door open.

"Is everything all right with the girls?"

"I believe so."

Keeping her hand on the door, she waited for him to explain why he was calling on her.

Lord Mountgarret appeared nervous as he wriggled the top hat in his hand. Then, his hands stilled.

"Are those my books?" he questioned, his eyes lingering on the books on the table.

"They are," she confirmed.

"May I ask why you stole my books?" he asked, his voice rising.

Unrattled by his sudden outburst, she clarified, "I *borrowed* them this morning. I have every intention of returning them when I'm finished."

His brows furrowed together. "Isn't borrowing something without asking the same as stealing?"

"A gentleman would say 'borrowing', my lord," she teased.

He held her gaze for several moments before asking, "May I speak to you for a moment?"

"Of course."

She exited the cottage and closed the door behind her.

"It's a lovely day. Would you care to go for a stroll?"

"What a fine idea," she replied, finding herself growing increasingly curious about why he was here.

He gestured that she should walk first. After they proceeded onto the footpath, he placed his hat on top of his head and said, "I wanted to thank you again for what you did last night."

"No thanks are necessary, my lord. I would do it again, if the situation arose."

"About that," he paused, clasping his hands behind his back, "I believe I was too hasty in firing you from your post."

"Is that so?"

He nodded. "Yes, and I would like to remedy that mistake, assuming you agree to certain terms."

"Which are?" she asked tentatively. Emeline had a suspicion that she was not going to like his terms.

Glancing over at her, he said, "I would like you to provide a more rigorous education for the girls and spend less time with the frivolous nonsense."

"Can you define the 'frivolous nonsense'?"

"I am speaking of idle time playing in the fields and searching for frogs."

"If I understand correctly," Emeline replied, keeping her face expressionless, "you are asking me to keep any and all fun out of the learning environment."

Lord Mountgarret's eyes scanned the fields surrounding Rumney Manor. "Surely, you must agree that idle time is not good for a young woman of good breeding."

"And you would know this… how?" she asked, attempting to keep the sarcasm out of her voice.

He frowned. "I have been charged with rearing these girls into women of worth, and not a moment should be wasted preparing them for Society."

"That's where I disagree with you." Emeline stopped and turned to face him. "These girls just lost their parents. They need time to adjust to their new life."

Appearing bored with her passionate plea, he said, "Those are my terms."

Taking a moment to study the infuriating lord, Emeline felt a twinge of pity for him. But not enough to stay under his employment.

"If those are your terms, then I'm afraid I must refuse your offer. Good day."

As she started to spin back around, Lord Mountgarret reached out and grabbed her arm. "I beg your pardon?"

"I wish you luck finding a governess for the girls, but it will not be me under those terms."

"And why not?" It was evident by his tone that he was a man who was used to getting what he wanted.

She gave him an exasperated look. "You want me to become something I am not in order to teach the girls your way. I refuse to change who *I* am to suit *your* needs."

"Who exactly are you, Miss Wren?" he asked dryly.

Emeline took a step closer to him. "I attended a prestigious boarding school, where I learned to speak multiple languages. I excel at embroidery, drawing, singing, dancing, and I am an accomplished rider. I daresay that my education has prepared me for the marriage mart."

"Yet, here you are, working as a governess." He lifted his brow.

Her eyes narrowed slightly. "You know nothing about me, Lord Mountgarret. You *think* you know me and my circumstances, but I assure you, you're wrong."

He put his hands up in front of him. "I haven't come here to fight with you. If you agree to my terms, I will increase your salary to £30 per year."

"Thank you, but I still must decline."

"I negotiate contracts for a living, Miss Wren. If you are attempting to extort me..."

She cut him off. "I'm doing no such thing. I am informing you that I'm not interested in your terms." She spun around and began walking away.

Lord Mountgarret's voice came from behind her. "£40!" he shouted.

Emeline shook her head as she continued walking the short distance back to the cottage. He just didn't seem to understand that money was not a motivating factor for her.

She had just stepped onto the porch when Lord Mountgarret's voice stopped her. It was gruff, but she heard a hint of a plea. "What will it take for you to stay on as governess to the girls?"

Turning back to face him, she gave him a tentative smile. "I want to be able to teach the girls on *my* terms."

"Unacceptable," he declared.

She reached to open the door of the cottage when he conceded. "Fine, but it will be on a trial basis."

"Agreed," she said. "I also want you to eat suppers as a family."

"We are not a family," he stated with his jaw tensed.

"You are, whether you care to admit it or not."

He let out an aggravated sigh. "I was planning to leave for London tomorrow."

She took a step towards him. "If I agree to stay on as governess, I will expect you to stay at Rumney Manor for at least the next week."

"A week! But I have..."

She spoke over him. "During the course of that week, you

will have supper with the girls, and spend time with them, getting to know them."

"I'm afraid I don't have the time…"

"Then good day," she interrupted, spinning back around towards the cottage.

She had just opened the door and taken a step inside when she heard Lord Mountgarret proclaim, "You win!"

"Pardon?"

He had an annoyed scowl on his face. "I will stay at Rumney Manor for a week, but I would like you in attendance when I spend time with the girls."

Frustrated by his pompous attitude, her eyes narrowed. "Do you think this is a game?" she accused. "Do you think I'm making impossible demands? Is it so wrong for a guardian to spend time with his wards?"

"Truly, I don't know what to think, Miss Wren." His words sounded sincere.

"You have two girls who are depending on you, Lord Mountgarret. You need to stand up and be there for them."

He tossed his hands up in the air. "I never asked for this responsibility."

"That doesn't matter," she countered. "You accepted guardianship of them. Now do right by them. Care for them as their father intended you to do."

As she watched him, for a moment she thought his eyes held a hint of vulnerability, but he blinked it away.

"I don't know what I am doing," he admitted.

She smirked. "That is painfully obvious." She took a step closer. "Truthfully, neither do I."

He huffed. "I sincerely doubt that."

"It's true," she insisted. "I've never been a governess before. I arrived at Rumney Manor to visit Mrs. Garvey, not to accept employment."

"If that was the case, then why did Mrs. Garvey hire you?"

Emeline gave a slight shrug of her shoulders. "The girls needed a governess when they arrived, and Mrs. Garvey offered me the position."

"But you're a natural with them, and they hate me."

"No, they don't hate you," she contended. "They don't know you."

Lord Mountgarret let out a deep, heartfelt sigh. "I agree to your terms. All of them."

"Thank you."

He considered her for a moment.

"You are a shrewd negotiator, Miss Wren," he finally said.

"I wasn't negotiating for myself… I was negotiating for the girls."

A glimmer of respect came to his eyes. "That you were, and you succeeded." He winced slightly as he looked towards Rumney Manor. "Would you mind starting now? The girls have been asking for you since breakfast."

"I suppose I could start now," she replied, "assuming I'm allowed to use your library for my personal use."

"Agreed," he said in a rush.

She smiled. "Inform the girls I'll be up shortly. I just want to grab a book from the pile that you let me *borrow* from your library."

"Thank you, Miss Wren," he said, his voice full of gratitude.

As Emeline stepped into the cottage, she picked up *Robinson Crusoe* from the pile and clutched it to her chest. She had a lot of work ahead of her if she was going to bridge the gap between Lord Mountgarret and his wards, especially since she only had two months to do it.

She'd better get to work!

7

"Why do we have to have supper with him?" Phoebe complained for what seemed liked the hundredth time.

Emeline just shook her head as she brushed Sophia's blonde tresses. "Lord Mountgarret is your guardian, and it's important for you to get to know one another."

"I don't want to get to know him," Phoebe contended. "He's mean."

Sophia nodded her agreement.

Putting the brush down, Emeline twisted Sophia's hair into a chignon and secured it with hairpins. "He is actually quite a pleasant man when you get to know him."

"Pleasant?" Phoebe questioned.

"Yes, he is."

Phoebe humphed. "I doubt that."

"You need to give Lord Mountgarret a chance," Emeline chided.

Phoebe crossed her arms over her chest. "Why should we give him a chance? He hired Mrs. Reid, and he fired you."

"True, but he did rehire me," she corrected. "That has to count for something."

The floor clock chimed, alerting them of the time.

"We are now officially late," she announced.

Phoebe mumbled, "Good."

Ignoring Phoebe's grumpy attitude, Emeline placed her hand out to Sophia. "It's not polite to make a gentleman wait longer than necessary."

They left the nursery and hurried down the stairs towards the dining room. As they stepped into the room, she saw Lord Mountgarret standing next to the fireplace with an annoyed look on his face.

"You're late," he commented.

She noticed that Sophia tightened her hold on her hand. "That we are," she stated with a smile. "It couldn't be helped."

He came closer to the table. "You are teaching the girls bad habits."

Dropping Sophia's hand, she encouraged her to be seated at the table before she walked up to Lord Mountgarret. She lowered her voice and admonished, "You're scowling."

"I am not."

She gave him a knowing look. "You are, and you're frightening the children."

His brow lifted in surprise. "I'm doing no such thing."

"Will you not attempt to be cordial?"

He huffed. "This may surprise you, but some people consider me charming."

"I am not one of those people."

Lord Mountgarret took a step back. "It appears we're starting off badly again, Miss Wren."

"Shall we start over… again?" she suggested.

A hint of a smile came to Lord Mountgarret's lips as he nodded.

Walking over to the table, Emeline waited as the footman pulled out her chair. She sat down, between the two girls, and reached for her napkin.

"Girls," she said, placing the napkin in her lap, "Lord Mountgarret would like to regale you with stories from his childhood."

"I would?" Lord Mountgarret asked as he sat down at the head of the table.

She nodded encouragingly. "You would."

A footman placed a bowl of soup in front of Lord Mountgarret as he shared, "I grew up at Rumney Manor. My father was rarely around... thankfully. But when he was, he was quite harsh. I was sent off to Eton College the moment I turned thirteen."

"What did you do for fun?" Emeline prodded.

He frowned. "My father would let me balance his ledgers with him. That was enjoyable."

If Emeline had been closer to Lord Mountgarret, she would have kicked him under the table. His stories were awful. She tried again.

"Did you have any friends?"

"I did. My cousin was my best friend. Her estate borders my property, and we grew up playing in the woodlands." His smiled dimmed. "That is, until her parents died in a horrible boating accident. She was sent off to boarding school."

Emeline was not prone to acts of violence, but her patience was growing increasingly thin with Lord Mountgarret.

"Before your cousin went to boarding school," she tried, "did you spend any time playing games?"

A smile came to his face, and Emeline relaxed a little. "We used to pretend to be pirates. Penelope insisted on being a female pirate, even though I told her they didn't exist." He grew pensive for a moment. "My uncle had a treehouse built for us that resembled a ship on his property. We would spend hours playing in the treehouse."

Sophia spoke up, her face brightening. "The treehouse looked like a ship?"

He nodded. "My uncle was rather fond of ships. He owned a merchant company."

"Which company was that?" Emeline asked.

Reaching for his spoon, he revealed, "Foster Company."

She stifled a gasp at his response. Did he truly just say "Foster Company"?

"Have you by chance heard of Warren Trading Company?"

"I believe most people have. They are one of our main rivals." He looked at her curiously. "Why do you ask?"

Emeline waved her hand dismissively, not wanting to share that her father owned that company.

"No reason," she replied lightly. She wasn't quite sure how Lord Mountgarret would act knowing that one of his main competitor's daughter was sitting at his table, dining with him and acting as a governess to his wards.

Lord Mountgarret turned his attention towards Sophia and asked, "What are some of your favorite pastimes?"

Sophia looked over at her for permission to speak.

Emeline smiled reassuringly.

Turning her face back towards Lord Mountgarret, Sophia replied, "I like to sing and play with dolls."

"Those are fine pastimes for a young lady to have," he remarked. "Do you like to play the pianoforte?"

She gave a shy smile. "I do."

"*Comment tu aimes tes leçons de Français?*" Lord Mountgarret asked.

"*Oui, beaucoup,*" Sophia replied, her smile growing.

Lord Mountgarret turned his attention towards Phoebe. "Are you enjoying your French lessons, as well?"

"Yes, my lord." Phoebe put her spoon down. "Miss Wren is most diligent when it comes to our lessons."

With an approving nod at Emeline, he returned his gaze to Phoebe. "And what about your pastimes?"

She wiped the sides of her mouth with her napkin. "I like to play with frogs and snakes."

He cleared his throat. "That's an interesting pastime. One that I am not sure I approve of."

"Sometimes I like to bring the reptiles back up with me into the nursery," she continued. "I keep them in my room as pets, at least until they escape."

"Escape?" Lord Mountgarret asked, his voice rising in disbelief.

She bobbed her head. "Then, I have to search through the halls for them. Once, I found a snake curled up in the library next to a cup of tea."

Sophia giggled. "Can you imagine a snake drinking tea?"

Emeline bit her lip to suppress the laugh that threatened to erupt at Sophia's imaginative idea.

With a tight jaw, Lord Mountgarret stated, "Do not bring reptiles into the estate again, young lady."

"But the snakes aren't poisonous, and the frogs are harmless," Phoebe argued.

"That is hardly the issue…"

At that moment, there was a loud croaking sound coming from Phoebe's side of the table. She brightened and asked, "Would you like to see my pet frog?"

Lord Mountgarret's mouth dropped. "Do you have a frog on your person?"

"I do. It's been in my pocket," she said, bringing her hand up from under the table and holding a large bullfrog. It croaked as it attempted to jump out of her hands.

Emeline's eyes widened as she reached to help Phoebe keep control of the large amphibian.

Frowning, Lord Mountgarret snapped his fingers at one of the footmen. "Please take the frog from Miss Phoebe and place it outside," he ordered.

Phoebe handed the frog to the footman and wiped her hands on her napkin.

Lord Mountgarret's fiery gaze snapped towards Emeline.

"May I speak to you for a moment, Miss Wren?" he said, shoving back his chair and tossing his napkin onto the table.

Emeline gave Phoebe a pointed look as she pushed her chair back. The girl had been goading Lord Mountgarret and had succeeded. In response, Phoebe attempted to appear innocent as she picked up her spoon and proceeded to eat her soup.

Emeline trailed behind Lord Mountgarret as he exited the dining room. Once they turned the corner, he spun around and stated, "A frog at the dinner table, Miss Wren?" His voice was low, hushed, and accusatory.

"I was as surprised as you were. Phoebe gave no indication that she intended to bring a frog to the table."

His eyes flashed with frustration. "I informed you earlier that it was wholly inappropriate for a young woman of good breeding to play with reptiles." He glanced down at the floor. "And now it appears that we have a snake loose somewhere in Rumney Manor."

Emeline shook her head. "Trust me, Phoebe was just goading you. She wanted a reaction, and she got it. Besides, frogs are amphibians, not reptiles."

"What?" he asked, confused, then waved his hand dismissively. "That's not the point. Why would she do that?"

Emeline shrugged one shoulder. "For fun?" she suggested. "She is only ten years old, after all."

"It must beg the question, what are you teaching her?"

Standing this close to Lord Mountgarret was rather unnerving. However, what surprised her the most was that she saw sadness lurking behind the anger in his eyes. What events in his life had caused him so much sadness?

Lord Mountgarret lifted his brow, and she realized that she had been caught staring. Speaking quickly, she shared, "I assure you that I will speak to Phoebe about bringing reptiles to the table."

"Or anywhere near Rumney Manor."

She tipped her head demurely. "Of course, my lord. Is there anything else?"

"Not at the moment," he said before brushing past her to walk back into the dining room.

Letting out a sigh, Emeline followed him back into the room, hoping the second course would be less eventful than the first.

The sun was just peeking over the horizon as Baldwin raced his horse near the woodlands of his estate. He loved to watch the sun rising higher in the sky, marking a new day. A new opportunity at life. It was also the perfect time to visit his mother's grave, without any distractions.

He took a moment to reflect on supper last night. It had been a disaster. After Phoebe pulled out the frog, they spent the rest of the time in awkward silence. Poor Miss Wren even attempted to extract conversation from them, but it was all for naught. None of them were feeling talkative.

His thoughts turned towards the governess. Miss Wren was an interesting young woman. She didn't appear docile as he would expect from someone in her position. Instead, she radiated confidence and optimism.

Exasperatingly.

Did that woman ever get discouraged? He didn't think it was possible.

Up ahead, in the woodlands, he saw someone racing their horse through the woods. Who could that be? It might be Penelope, but he didn't think they'd arrived yet. Forgetting his plan to visit his mother's grave, he turned his horse towards the woodlands and urged it into a run.

As he raced closer, he saw the female rider slide off an unfamiliar grey gelding near a stream. The rising sun sent shafts of brilliant light through the branches overhead, providing him with enough light to make out Miss Wren, dressed in a blue riding habit.

He slowed his horse's gait and approached her. "Is that your horse, Miss Wren?"

Taking her hand, she ran it lovingly along the gelding's neck. "It is," she confirmed. "I brought him with me."

He paused. What governess had the funds at her disposal to own a horse?

Mistaking his silence for disapproval, Miss Wren said, "Mrs. Garvey gave me permission to board my horse at your stables. If that is a problem, then I am more than happy to pay for my horse's keep out of my salary…"

Holding up his hand, he silenced her. "You're welcome to board your horse at my stables."

"Thank you," she responded, gifting him with a bright smile. A smile that he wouldn't mind seeing again.

He glanced over his shoulder and asked, "Did you not bring an escort with you?"

"No. I assumed it would be safe if I stayed on your land."

"You're correct. Although, I must urge you to be cautious riding through these woodlands."

She cocked her head. "Have you always been such a killjoy?"

"Me? A killjoy?" he repeated in surprise.

There was an amused twinkle in Miss Wren's eye when she replied, "You're always so quick to criticize and reprimand."

Adjusting the reins in his hands, he replied defensively, "I'm merely stating a fact. These woods can be quite treacherous, especially after an early morning rain shower."

"As I told you before, I am a proficient rider."

"I must admit that was evident by the way you navigated through the trees."

She eyed him suspiciously. "Did you just compliment me?"

"I believe I did," he said with a wry smile.

Miss Wren stepped closer to the stream and picked up a leaf. She began twirling it between her fingers. "Last night, when you spoke of your father, you seemed resentful of him."

"That's true. My father was a blackguard."

She arched an eyebrow. "That sounds rather harsh."

"Not if you'd ever met the man in person," he shared. "He gambled away the family fortune, many times over. He seduced members of his own household staff, and he maintained many mistresses over the years."

"Sadly, your father is not much different than most of the men in Society," she muttered under her voice.

He pointed at the ground. "May I join you?" he asked, seeking her permission.

"Of course," she replied, dropping the leaf to the ground.

Dismounting, he led his horse to the stream for a drink. "My father was a drunk most of his life. He beat my mother, and he resented me."

"How could he resent you?" she questioned. "You were the heir."

He kicked at a rock near the stream's edge, watching as it took flight. "I was never good enough for him. He would tell me frequently how ignorant and incompetent I was. Once, he even told me that I was a bastard, and I wasn't truly his son."

"Was that true?"

He shook his head. "My mother swore that she was never unfaithful. I have no reason to doubt her, whereas my father was a compulsive liar."

"Your father sounds cruel."

He scoffed. "He was. He kept slinging the same insults at me, and over time, I started believing them."

She gave him a sad smile. "That sounds awful."

"It was. But when my father was absent from Rumney Manor, which was quite frequently, my uncle stepped in and filled the void of a father figure. He spent time with me and encouraged me to be diligent in my coursework." He grew silent before adding, "He even told me that if I worked hard, then one day, I would own a part of Foster Company."

"That was rather generous of him."

"It was," he agreed. "I mourned his life dearly, but I felt nothing when my own father died."

"That's to be expected under the circumstances," she remarked.

He glanced curiously over at her. "When did your father pass?"

"My father isn't dead," she replied, looking startled by her own admission.

"My apologies, I had assumed because you are working as a governess..."

She grew quiet as she turned her direction upstream. "My situation required me to leave my home. It was never my intention to work as a governess, but I must admit that I have found enjoyment in it."

"Have you always been this cheery?" he found himself asking.

She gave him a baffled look. "I have been called many things in my life, but never 'cheery'."

"I'm impressed by your outlook on life," he said. "Even in your reduced circumstances, you still find joy."

"Why would I not?"

"A woman of your station clearly would prefer to be married than working for an income."

He watched her shoulders as they squared.

"And what would you say if I told you that I willingly chose to be a governess?"

"I would say that you are fabricating a lie. No woman would willingly work if they did not have to."

She met his gaze, her eyes full of determination. "Not all women aspire to marry."

"Why would a woman not want the security of marriage?" he asked, baffled.

Miss Wren stepped out onto a large rock in the middle of the stream. She turned back towards him. "I wish to marry for love."

"I see that you've been reading fairy tales," he said in a mocking chide.

"Perhaps," came her simple reply, "but I don't intend to settle for anything less."

"Is that why you chose spinsterhood then?"

Placing a hand on her hip, she countered, "You know very little about me, Lord Mountgarret. Your assumptions are doing you a disservice."

He held his hands up. "Then please enlighten me. Who is Miss Wren?"

She gave him an exasperated look. "You insult me, repeatedly, then ask me to confide in you." Stepping over to the other side of the stream, she picked up a smooth rock and fingered it in her hands. "I may be employed by you, but I have a right to maintain my own privacy."

"You do," he replied. "I was merely making conversation."

Tossing the rock into the stream, she said, "I would prefer to speak of the weather."

He chuckled, amused by her response. "I had not taken you for someone that likes to engage in polite conversation."

She watched him curiously. "This is the first time that I've seen you laugh."

"That's not true."

"It is," she replied. "It suits you."

His eyes scanned the trees as he admitted, "For so long, I was miserable, but now I have reasons to smile in my life. I finally have hope."

"What changed?"

"My reduced circumstances, actually," he shared. "My cousin and her new husband paid off my outstanding debts, repaired Rumney Manor, and brought me on as a partner of Foster Company."

"That was kind of them."

He nodded. "It was. Because of them, I have a new start at life."

"A new start sounds wonderful," she murmured.

In her words, he detected vulnerability. He studied her for a moment, then asked, "What are you running from, Miss Wren?"

"Running? I'm not running from anything," she insisted.

Baldwin lifted his brow at the urgency in her voice. "Everyone is running from something," he prodded.

Miss Wren wasn't forthcoming in her response, so he watched as a squirrel ran up a birch tree and into a cavity near the base. The squirrel then popped his head out and ran back down the tree once again.

"It's time for me to go check on the girls," she announced before she crossed the stream at a fast pace.

He stepped to the left side of her horse and clasped his fingers together. "Allow me," he said.

She placed her hands on his shoulders, slipped her boot into his hands, and allowed him to assist her onto her side-saddle.

After she was securely seated on the horse, she began adjusting the skirt of her riding habit. "Thank you."

He placed a hand on her horse's neck. "Why do I feel as if you are running from me?"

"I am not," she proclaimed. "Did you forget that my first priority is to care for the girls?"

"Ah, I see that you are finally starting to take your role as governess seriously," he observed, stepping back.

She let out an amused huff. "You are truly a vexing man, Lord Mountgarret."

"Will I see you at supper tonight?"

"Yes, and I will ensure that Phoebe does not bring along another visitor."

He bowed. "Until tonight, then."

Baldwin watched as she turned her horse back towards the path and urged it into a run. Miss Wren had secrets. He found that fascinating. What was she hiding from? Did she become a governess to avoid a loveless marriage?

Either way, he would get her to confide in him.

8

THE SUN WAS HIGH, AND THE BIRDS WERE CHIRPING OUTSIDE THE window of Baldwin's study. He sat at his desk with a note from Thomas's solicitor in his hand. He had already read it multiple times, but his eyes scanned over the words again.

LORD MOUNTGARRET,

A RELATIVE OF MISS PHOEBE AND MISS SOPHIA HAS COME forward to request guardianship. With your approval, I shall accompany Mr. and Mrs. Stewart to Rumney Manor to discuss the matter.

THANK YOU,
   Mr. Walter Baker

. . .

Baldwin should feel elated by this news. After all, this was a solution to his problem. Instead, he felt deflated. Could he truly just hand the girls over to Mr. and Mrs. Stewart and be done with them? That's not what his friend wanted, but perhaps that was what was best for the girls.

He knew firsthand the hurt associated with being stripped away from someone's family. Because of his father's despicable reputation, Penelope had been kept hidden away at Miss Bell's Finishing School. It was nearly four years before he saw her again. Could he be the one responsible for keeping the girls away from their family?

For the past three days, he'd had minimal interaction with the girls during the day, focusing solely on work, but they had come together for supper every evening. During these meals, the girls hardly said a word, while Miss Wren filled the void by chatting incessantly. It was vexing and charming at the same time. She somehow made the most uneventful tasks seem exciting.

"Lord Mountfarret," a little girl said from the doorway.

He turned in his chair to see Sophia standing at the doorway. "It's Mountgarret," he corrected.

"Oh," she replied, looking down at her feet. "May I hide in your study?"

"I beg your pardon?"

Glancing over her shoulder, she said, "We're playing hide and seek, and I'm trying to hide from Miss Wren."

"And you think my study is an appropriate place to hide?"

She nodded. "Miss Wren would never look for me in here."

"That's true, but only because no one is allowed in my study but me."

A crestfallen expression came to her face. "I'm sorry, Lord Mountmarret." She turned to leave.

Touched by her sad face, he said, "Wait." He waved her closer. "First of all, my name is Mount-*garret*." She stopped at his desk. "Can you say that?"

"Mountgarret," she repeated, scrunching her nose. "Why is your name so long?"

"That's my title. I am the Viscount of Mountgarret."

"I suppose that isn't too long. My name is Barrington and that's quite long, too."

"True."

He took a moment to study the little girl with blonde hair. She had soft features and a round, youthful face. "Normally, my study is forbidden to everyone, but I will make an exception this one time."

Sophia jumped in excitement. "Oh, thank you, Lord Mountgarret."

He tilted his head towards the maroon drapes framing the windows. "Why don't you go hide behind those drapes?"

She nodded enthusiastically and rushed over to hide behind the drapes. He smiled as he noticed that the tips of her boots were showing.

He walked closer to the window and asked, "How long do you suppose it will take Miss Wren to find you?"

He heard her muffled reply, "It could be hours. This is a really good hiding spot."

"Hours?" He chuckled. "Should I order your midday meal to be sent to here?"

Giggling, she replied, "Miss Wren will find me before then."

"What if she doesn't?" he pressed. "What if you are forced to sleep all night behind those drapes?"

Sophia's head peeked out from behind the drapes. "I don't want to sleep here all night. Should I find an easier hiding spot?"

He shrugged. "It's up to you, but I once stayed a whole week behind the drapes when I was hiding from my cousin."

"A whole week?"

"Yes, it was a very long week."

Sophia looked at him in astonishment. "You are truly the best hider I've ever met."

Before he could reply, Baldwin heard Miss Wren calling for Sophia from the entry hall.

"Miss Wren is coming. You need to hide," he informed the girl.

Sophia stuck her head back behind the drape just as Miss Wren walked into the room. She was dressed in a white gown with a green sash around her waist. He found it curious that she dressed more like a debutante than a governess. But he had to admit that he preferred it.

"I'm sorry to disturb you, Lord Mountgarret, but I am trying to find Sophia," she said.

"You lost Sophia?" he shouted.

She winced. "Not exactly."

"What does that mean?"

Walking further into the room, she revealed, "We're playing a hiding game, and I can't seem to find her."

"I see," he said, clasping his hands behind his back. "Where have you looked?"

"The library, the drawing room, the nursery, and the kitchen."

"But not the stables?"

"No, Sophia is wise enough not to leave the manor."

Unclasping his hands, he pointed towards the drapes that Sophia was hiding behind. "Have you tried looking in any of the guest rooms?"

Nodding her understanding, Miss Wren slowly walked closer to the drapes. "I have not."

"Well, let's hope you find Sophia before her midday meal," he said. "I would hate for her to go hungry because she was in such a brilliant hiding spot."

Playing along, Miss Wren continued, "It would be a shame, because the cook has promised the girls biscuits with their meals."

"Biscuits?" he repeated.

"Yes, but I'm not sure if Sophia likes biscuits."

A muffled voice came from behind the drapes. "She does."

Miss Wren stifled a smile. "Did you hear that? It sounded like it was coming from behind the drapes."

"I did, but whatever could it be?" he teased.

Closing the distance in a few strides, Miss Wren tossed back the drapes to reveal Sophia. "I found you."

Sophia beamed up at her. "You did, but it took you a really long time."

"That's true, but only because you cheated," Miss Wren said. "You know you're not allowed to be in Lord Mountgarret's study, for any reason."

Sophia looked at the floor, suddenly dejected.

Miss Wren went and crouched down in front of the girl. "What do you say to Lord Mountgarret?"

The girl looked up at him with wide, saddened eyes. "I'm sorry for disturbing you."

"No harm done," he replied gently.

Miss Wren rose and extended her hand towards Sophia. "If you will excuse us, we will continue our game on the second level."

As they began walking towards the door, he surprised himself by saying, "For future reference, I am not opposed to occasionally opening up my study for a rousing game of hide and seek."

Miss Wren stopped and turned back with an astonished look on her face. "That is most gracious of you, my lord."

"Nonsense," he replied. "Besides, there are very few good hiding spots at Rumney Manor."

Sophia smiled broadly at him. "Thank you, Lord Mountgarret."

"You are most welcome, Miss Sophia," he replied as he returned her smile. "If you're not opposed, perhaps I can show you my favorite hiding spot."

Sophia turned her gaze towards Miss Wren. "Can he, Miss Wren?"

Miss Wren nodded.

Walking over to the wall, he pushed on the panel to reveal a servant's passage. "Rumney Manor has servant's passages all over the estate."

Sophia dropped Miss Wren's hand and ran over to the passage. She stepped inside and closed the panel.

He chuckled. "She might be in there for a while."

Miss Wren approached him. "That was most kind of you."

"I am not a complete monster, regardless of what you may think of me."

"I never said you were a 'monster'," she corrected, "but I may have implied you didn't like to have fun."

"May have? I believe you called me a 'killjoy'," he reminded her. "Besides, there is a time and a place for having fun."

"When is the appropriate time to have fun?"

"I suppose after your work is done."

Glancing over at his desk, she asked, "Have you completed your work for the day?"

"I have enough work to last me two lifetimes."

"So, when do you have fun?"

"I go riding in the morning," he informed her. "That is most assuredly fun."

"Do you hunt?"

"Occasionally."

"When in Town, do you attend the theatre?"

"Rarely."

"Have you ever gone to the Royal Menagerie?"

He shook his head. "I have not."

"Pity. The beasts are enjoyable to watch." She took a step closer to him. "Please say that you have watched the fireworks at Vauxhall Gardens."

"No, but I have watched them from my office."

She brushed the brown curls away from her face. "That's not the same thing."

Leaning back against his desk, he said, "I don't have time…"

"To have fun," she answered for him.

He pressed his lips together. "I was going to say that I don't have idle time to waste." He tapped his finger on his desk. "Have you been to all those places in Town?"

She nodded. "I have."

He humphed.

"What?"

He met her gaze. "I am just trying to make sense of you. That's all."

"Does it surprise you that I had a life before I became a governess?" she asked with an arched eyebrow.

"I guess not." He studied her for a moment before asking, "Did you have a Season?"

"Three, in fact."

"I'm surprised you received no offers."

Her lips parted in surprise. "I received many offers, and it's not very gentlemanly of you to assume otherwise."

Baldwin opened his mouth to apologize when the panel in the wall slid open, and Sophia stepped out, smiling. "These passageways are brilliant. I have to show Phoebe."

"I thought you might enjoy them," Baldwin remarked. "But you must promise to never listen in on anyone's conversation."

"I promise," she replied quickly.

Miss Wren reached her hand out to Sophia. "Come, Sophia."

As they started walking towards the door, Baldwin spoke up. "Wait, Miss Wren."

With a rigid back, Miss Wren slowly turned towards him. "Yes, Lord Mountgarret."

"I'm sorry for what I just said."

Some of the tension drained from her shoulders as she

replied, "Thank you for that." Turning on her heel, she quickly left the room.

Sitting down in his chair, Baldwin watched the doorway for a long moment. He couldn't make sense of Miss Wren. She clearly came from privilege. So how did she end up working as a governess? Every time he got too close, she became guarded and would flee from his presence. He needed a new strategy.

No, he needed to focus on work and stop thinking of the lovely Miss Wren. Besides, he had a letter to write.

Baldwin knew he was scowling as he sorted through the many ledgers on his desk. Usually, he enjoyed this mundane task, but he was growing tired of the ever-growing pile of work he had to accomplish. He needed to go back to London to complete the tasks, but he promised Miss Wren that he would stay for a week.

A whole week.

He wasn't entirely sure why. It wasn't as if his wards were fond of him. Truth be told, they barely tolerated him. But they loved Miss Wren. Who wouldn't? She was always smiling and sharing stories about her childhood. Fortunately, his time was almost up. He intended to depart for London in the morning and be free of his wards and their infuriatingly cheerful governess.

A familiar voice came from the doorway. "I know that look," Nicholas, the Duke of Blackbourne, said. "You're glowering."

"Glowering?" he repeated. "I am not."

Penelope walked into the room. "You are, cousin. In fact, you could scare little children with that scowl."

He closed the ledger in front of him. "If you must know, I have spent all morning reviewing the ledgers of Foster Company."

Walking around to a velvet settee, Penelope sat down. "How is our company doing?"

"Very well."

"That's wonderful news. Then you deserve a break," Penelope stated.

"A break?" He chuckled. "I don't think so. There is always work to be done."

Penelope lifted her brow. "When Nicholas informed me that you had returned to your estate, I was surprised. You'd previously announced that you were going to spend the fall in London."

"That had been the plan."

Nicholas went and sat down next to his wife. "May I ask what happened?"

"If you must know, Miss Wren requested that I remain at Rumney Manor for a week."

"Who is Miss Wren?" Penelope asked.

"The girls' governess," he explained.

Nicholas gave him a curious look. "Since when did a governess dictate your actions?"

"It's a long story," he huffed. "However, Miss Wren thought that it would be prudent if I spent a week getting to know my wards."

"I must admit that I agree with your governess," Nicholas said, nodding.

"You do?"

"It is a good thing to develop a relationship with your wards," Nicholas contended.

"I suppose so."

"How are your wards adjusting to Rumney Hall?" Penelope asked.

He picked up a few sheets of paper and moved them to the side of his desk. "They hate me."

"They hate you?" Penelope repeated, sounding surprised.

He nodded.

Nicholas laughed. "There could be many reasons for that."

Ignoring his friend's comment, Baldwin said, "I try to engage with them, but I feel like I'm making no progress. The older girl, Phoebe, even brought a frog to the dinner table to irritate me."

"A frog?" Penelope questioned, attempting to hide her smile. "That's ingenious."

Baldwin leaned back in his chair. "I don't know what I'm doing wrong."

Nicholas rose and walked over to the drink cart. "Children are crafty creatures. You must establish dominance, or they will assert their power, making you powerless."

"Miss Wren said I should love them," he argued.

"You can love them, but still be firm with them," Nicholas said, taking the stopper off the decanter. "Children need discipline. It is just like my crew on the HMS *Victorious*..."

Baldwin groaned. "Not another one of your Navy stories."

Pouring himself a drink, Nicholas replied, "You may gripe, but there was a reason why I was such a successful captain in His Majesty's Royal Navy."

"I, for one, am excited to meet your wards," Penelope said.

Rising, Baldwin sighed. "You shall see firsthand how little they hold me in regard." He walked over to the doorway and called, "Drake!"

His butler walked across the entry hall. "Yes, milord."

"Can you inform Miss Wren that my wards' presence is required in my study?"

He tipped his head. "As you wish."

Walking over to the drink cart, Baldwin poured himself a drink and went and sat down across from Penelope.

"How are you faring?" he asked.

She smiled. "I'm well. In fact, we just learned that I am with child."

"Congratulations," he replied. "What wonderful news!"

Penelope placed her hand over her stomach. "We're pleased, and Nicholas's mother was overjoyed to hear the news."

"I have no doubt that my mother will dote on the child." Nicholas's eyes were full of pride as he looked at his wife.

He took a sip of his drink. "I'm glad, cousin. You deserve to be happy."

"As do you," she pressed.

"I am."

"Are you?"

He eyed her curiously. "Yes. Why would you think otherwise?"

Penelope moved to sit on the edge of her seat. "Partially because I never saw you at any social gatherings or balls this past Season."

"I was busy," he defended.

"Too busy to find a wife?" Nicholas asked.

Placing his empty glass on the table, Baldwin replied, "A wife is overrated."

"I could not disagree more," Nicholas contended.

A knock came at the door, and Miss Wren walked in with Phoebe and Sophia. They were both dressed in white frocks, and their hair was nicely coiffed.

"Thank you for coming so quickly, Miss Wren," Baldwin said, rising from his chair.

"You're welcome…"

"Emeline?" Penelope asked, rising from her chair.

Miss Wren looked at Penelope with confusion on her face before it broke out into a broad smile. "Penelope?" She rushed over and the two women embraced. "What are you doing here?"

"What am *I* doing here? What are *you* doing here?" Penelope asked.

"I'm the governess."

"You, a governess?" Penelope repeated. "Did something happen to your father?"

With a side-glanced towards Baldwin, Miss Wren murmured, "May I speak to you privately?"

Penelope nodded. "You may, Miss *Wren*," she replied in an amused tone. "But first allow me to introduce you to my husband, Nicholas, the Duke of Blackbourne."

Nicholas bowed. "Miss Wren, it is a pleasure to meet you."

Miss Wren curtsied. "Likewise, your grace." She turned her gaze towards Baldwin. "Would it be possible to leave the girls with you for a moment, my lord?"

"With me? Alone?" Baldwin asked.

Miss Wren looked disappointed by his response. "It will only be for a moment while I speak to Penelope privately."

Nicholas spoke up. "It would be his privilege."

"Thank you, your grace," Miss Wren said, looping her arm through Penelope's. "I shall only borrow your wife for a few moments."

Baldwin watched as Miss Wren and Penelope exited the room, still reeling from learning that his cousin was friends with his governess. Apparently, good friends, at that!

Now, he was left alone with his wards. Well, not quite alone. Nicholas was there, and he appeared to be trying to stifle a grin. Baldwin turned his gaze towards the girls, and they appeared as uncomfortable with the situation as he felt. He decided he should make the introductions.

"Your grace, allow me to introduce you to my wards, Miss Phoebe and Miss Sophia."

Nicholas bowed. "It is a pleasure to meet you both."

In response, Phoebe and Sophia executed flawless curtsies, but their gazes remained downcast.

"Phoebe is ten," he gestured towards her, "and Sophia is eight."

An awkward silence filled the room as Nicholas looked at him expectedly. In an attempt to make conversation, he shared, "Phoebe likes frogs, and Sophia likes to play hide and seek."

"You like frogs?" Nicholas asked, turning his gaze towards Phoebe.

"I do," she replied softly.

"What do you like about them?"

Phoebe shrugged. "They're slimy."

"I would agree with you there." Nicholas turned his attention toward Sophia. "Where is your favorite place to hide?"

Sophia met his gaze. "In the servant's passageway. May I show you?"

"You may," the duke replied.

With slow steps, she walked over to the panel in the wall and slid it over. "This was also Lord Mountgarret's favorite place to hide when he was younger."

"It was?" Nicholas asked, feigning surprise.

Sophia bobbed her head energetically. "May I show my sister, Phoebe?"

"You may," he answered.

"Come look, Phoebe," Sophia encouraged, waving her over.

In the next moment, Phoebe and Sophia disappeared into the servant's passageway. Nicholas turned towards him. "That was awful."

"That bad?"

Nicholas grimaced. "I have seen prisoners of war receiving better reception from their enemies than what you just showed your wards."

"It wasn't *that* bad."

"It was terrible. You were entirely too stiff."

Baldwin tossed his head back and looked at the ceiling. "I don't know the first thing about rearing children. I've been trying to tell you that."

"Neither do I," he challenged. "But children can sense weakness."

"I'm not weak."

"I never said you were, but you become very unsure of yourself around them."

"I daresay you couldn't do any better."

A smile came to Nicholas's face. "Challenge accepted." He walked over to the passageway and ordered, "Miss Phoebe and Miss Sophia, come here, please."

Tentatively, his wards walked out of the passageway and looked up at Nicholas with uncertainty in their eyes.

Nicholas stood in front of them and proclaimed, "From now on, you are a part of my crew."

The girls' eyes grew wide, but they didn't say anything.

"Do either of you girls know how to swab the deck?"

They shook their heads.

"Sail a ship?"

Again, they shook their heads.

He feigned disappointment. "Can you at least sword fight?"

"No, your grace," they mumbled their disappointment.

"That *must* change," the duke stated. "We shall practice sword fighting on the lawn."

A pout came to Sophia's lips. "I don't think Miss Wren would let us play with swords."

Nicholas rubbed his chin thoughtfully. "I believe you're right. After all, you are a little too young to play with real swords. Perhaps we should scour the woodlands and find long sticks you can practice with instead."

The girls nodded enthusiastically.

"All right, but I don't want any dilly-dallying. I run a tight ship," he declared.

"No, your grace," they shouted energetically.

He nodded in approval. "Excellent. You will make fine additions to my crew."

With a newfound twinkle in their eyes, the girls smiled up at Nicholas. Sophia was so excited that she was practically jumping up and down.

"Come on, crew!" Nicholas shouted as he turned towards the door. "There is much work to be done if you are to be prepared to face the enemy."

Baldwin stood rooted in his spot as he watched his wards eagerly follow the duke. How did Nicholas manage to win the girls over so quickly?

Nicholas stopped at the door and looked back at him. "Are you coming, Baldwin?" he asked with a smug grin on his face.

"I wouldn't miss this for the world," he replied.

9

Without saying a word, Emeline led Penelope towards the drawing room. It wasn't until she closed the door that she turned to face her friend and asked, "You married your guardian?"

Penelope nodded. "I did."

Emeline walked further into the room. "Based on your descriptions of him when we were at school, I'd always imagined the duke to be a hairy man with missing teeth."

Laughing, Penelope sat on a velvet settee. "That would have been the previous duke. Nicholas inherited guardianship of me when he became the duke."

"He's quite handsome."

"He is. I find I'm partial to him," Penelope joked.

"I'm glad." She smiled. "Was it love at first sight?"

"Heavens, no. We fell in love gradually."

"I am truly happy for you."

Placing a hand on her stomach, Penelope shared, "I am increasing."

Emeline clasped her hands in front of her. "How exciting! Congratulations!"

"Thank you." Penelope gave her a knowing look. "Do you want to explain how you came to be a governess at my cousin's estate? And under an assumed name, no less."

"Your cousin?" she groaned. "That means that *you* own Foster Company. How did I not realize that?"

"That was a well-guarded secret when we were at school," the duchess shared. "I didn't want anyone to treat me differently."

"That makes logical sense. I did the same thing."

"You did?"

She pressed her lips together. "My father owns Warren Trading Company."

Penelope's brows shot up. "He does?"

Emeline nodded.

"Then, how did you come to work as a governess?"

Coming to sit down next to her, Emeline started, "If you recall, last time I saw you, I left Miss Bell's Finishing School to prepare for the Season with my stepmother."

"I remember."

"For the past three Seasons, I have participated in the dreaded marriage mart looking for a husband."

Penelope gave her a baffled look. "You haven't received any offers during three Seasons?"

"Why does everyone always assume that? I've received offers," she said, rising. "I received plenty of offers, but none that I truly considered."

"Were these advantageous offers?"

"Many were."

"But…" Penelope said, her voice trailing off.

Wincing, Emeline admitted, "I know this may sound ridiculous to you, but I want to marry for love."

Penelope smiled. "I think that's wonderful."

"You do?"

"Jo, Carolina, and Adelaide made a similar promise to each other, and we all married for love."

"That does give me hope," Emeline murmured. "However, my stepmother does not share my sentiments. She even accused me of sabotaging my younger stepsister's chance for finding a suitable match."

"In what way?"

"Until I accept an offer, it's inappropriate for any man to show interest in her."

Penelope lifted her brow. "There are exceptions to that rule."

"Not according to my stepmother," Emeline lamented. "After we returned back to our estate, she demanded that I accept an offer from Lord Mortain."

"What was wrong with him?"

"Nothing, except he is my father's age."

Penelope giggled. "I see the problem."

"Besides, I refuse to marry a man who is more interested in my embroidery skills than my opinions."

"I agree with you there."

Walking over to the window, Emeline peered out and shared, "I overheard my stepmother telling my horrid stepsister that she intended to lock me in my bedchamber until I agreed to Lord Mortain's courtship."

"How awful."

"It gets worse," she shared.

"How can it get worse?"

She wrapped her arms around her waist. "If locking me in my bedchamber didn't work, then my stepmother planned to have me committed to Bedlam."

"But you aren't mad!" Penelope exclaimed in astonishment.

"That didn't matter to her. She's cruel and conniving. Furthermore, she said she had already found two doctors to support her claim."

Penelope drew her eyebrows together in question. "What does your father say about all this?"

"He's gone," she declared.

"Gone where?"

"The West Indies," she answered. "After he married my stepmother, he started traveling all the time for business. This time, he's been gone for eight months."

"Eight months? That's a long time."

"It is, and I miss him dearly." Uncrossing her arms, she came to sit down next to Penelope. "After I overheard my stepmother's plan, I knew I needed to leave Cairnwood Hall, at least until my twenty-first birthday."

"What happens on your twenty-first birthday?"

"I will inherit my grandmother's estate, and I will have sufficient funds to rent a cottage and hire on a few servants. If I'm frugal with my funds, I shall never have to work for an income."

Penelope studied her for a moment. "That still doesn't explain how you became a governess," she pressed.

"The lead groomsman at my ancestral estate is a dear friend, and his sister, Mrs. Garvey, is Lord Mountgarret's housekeeper. When I arrived at Rumney Manor, I discovered they were in desperate need of a governess for the girls, and I was hired on the spot. She was the one who suggested I should change my name to Miss Wren."

Penelope frowned. "You can't keep working as a governess."

"Why not?"

"If anyone ever discovered your identity, it could ruin your reputation."

She nibbled her bottom lip. "I'm only working here for two months, under an assumed name. I don't believe anyone will discover my deceit."

"Why not come work for me as a companion?" Penelope suggested. "My last companion left after only a few weeks."

"As tempting as that offer is, I'm afraid I can't leave the girls now."

Penelope's face softened at her admission. "You truly care for them, don't you?"

"I do."

"Fine, I'll keep your secret, but that's only because you are making my cousin go mad," Penelope teased.

"In what way?"

Penelope smiled. "How did you convince him to stay at Rumney Manor for a whole week?"

"That was easy," she admitted. "He fired me after our first meeting because of my impertinence. However, when he attempted to hire me back, I had conditions."

"You had conditions?"

"I did. I wanted him to stay at Rumney Manor for a whole week and spend time getting to know his wards."

"How is he doing with the girls?"

Emeline brought her hand up to hide her growing smile. "Awful."

"That bad?"

She nodded. "Your cousin has a kind heart, but he hides it behind a gruff exterior."

"That's a fair assessment."

"The older girl, Phoebe, brought a frog to the dinner table just to goad him."

"Oh, dear heavens," Penelope said, her hand flying to her heart.

"On the other hand, he's winning Sophia over just by spending time with her."

"My cousin has never been around little children before," Penelope shared.

Emeline smiled. "That is painfully obvious."

"Does Baldwin know that you only intend to stay on as the governess until your twenty-first birthday?"

"It hasn't come up," she replied, pressing her lips together.

"It hasn't come up?" Penelope repeated in astonishment. "Don't you think he has a right to know that you intend to leave in less than two months?"

"I suppose I should tell him."

"I would, and the sooner the better."

A knock came at the door. A young serving maid opened it and entered holding a tray. "Mrs. Garvey thought you might like tea and biscuits, your grace."

"That was most thoughtful of her," Penelope replied.

The maid placed the tray on the table in front of the duchess. "Would you like me to pour you a cup?"

Penelope shook her head. "That's not necessary, but thank you."

The maid curtsied and departed without saying another word.

Emeline sat on the edge of her chair. "Allow me," she said, picking up the teapot and pouring two cups of tea.

"Frankly, I am surprised we didn't run into each other in town," the duchess said, accepting a cup of tea from Emeline. "It would have been fun to go shopping with you."

"I'm not," she replied. "After all, my family does not associate with the elite of Society."

"You do now. Next time you come into London, you shall accompany me to a social gathering of your choosing," Penelope stated.

"Perhaps a ball at Almack's," Emeline suggested as she took a sip of her tea.

The sound of children laughing drifted through the opened windows. Placing their cups on the tray, the women rose from their seats, and walked over to see who was making the noise.

The sight of Phoebe and Sophia sparring with sticks on the lawn with Lord Mountgarret and the duke brought a wide smile to Emeline's face.

"Should we join them?" she asked playfully.

Penelope smiled. "I think that sounds like a brilliant idea."

Standing in the center of the nursery, Phoebe huffed, "Why do we have to have dinner with him *again*?"

"Need I remind you yet again that Lord Mountgarret is your guardian? He's attempting to get to know you," Emeline explained as she pinned back Sophia's hair.

"He hardly says anything to us," Phoebe complained.

Sophia spoke up. "I like Lord Mountgarret. He's nice."

"You only think he is nice because he let you hide in his study today," Phoebe argued.

"That's not true," Sophia replied. "He also pretended to be a pirate today when we were fencing on the lawn. I ran him through… twice."

"His grace told me that I was an excellent sword fighter," Phoebe shared as she puffed out her little chest with pride.

"I must admit that you both are naturals," Emeline praised.

"Can we practice with real swords tomorrow?" Sophia asked eagerly.

She shook her head. "Absolutely not. You are much too young for that."

"I told you," Phoebe said, crossing her arms over her chest.

Rising from her chair, Emeline ran her eyes down the length of Phoebe. "Do you have a frog on your person?"

"No."

"A snake, perhaps?"

Phoebe shook her head. "Truthfully, I don't even like snakes."

"What about a furry rodent?"

Phoebe gave her an exasperated look. "I don't have anything on me."

"I just have to make sure, after the frog episode," Emeline responded with a smile.

A knock came at the nursery door, and she crossed the room in a few strides. When she opened the door, she saw Lord Mountgarret, finely dressed, standing on the other side.

She curtsied. "Good evening, Lord Mountgarret."

"Good evening, Miss Wren," he replied. "I was hoping to walk my wards down to dinner tonight."

"What a great honor," she acknowledged, giving Phoebe an expectant look. "What do you say to Lord Mountgarret?"

Phoebe stepped forward and curtsied. "Thank you, Lord Mountgarret."

With a kind smile, he said, "That was nicely done, Phoebe."

Lord Mountgarret stepped into the room and offered his arm. Phoebe tentatively placed her hand on his arm. He started to offer his other arm to Sophia, but she instead slipped her hand into his. Rather than chide her on her breach of etiquette, he just smiled down at her.

As they walked down the hall, Lord Mountgarret remarked, "The Duke and Duchess of Blackbourne have asked us to visit with them tomorrow at their estate, Brighton Hall. Penelope is eager to show you the underground grotto. It's lined with shells."

"What's a grotto?" Sophia asked.

Emeline answered, "It's like a cave."

"Oh, I like caves," Sophia murmured.

"Do you think we can practice sword fighting again with his grace?" Phoebe asked.

"I don't see why not, especially since we saved your long sticks," Lord Mountgarret replied.

Sophia smiled up at Lord Mountgarret. "His grace is nice."

" 'Nice'," he repeated. "I have never heard anyone refer to his grace as 'nice'."

"What would you refer to him as?" Phoebe asked.

Lord Mountgarret chuckled. "I might not be the right person

to ask. He once accused me of nefarious intentions towards my cousin."

"What does 'nefarious' mean?" Sophia questioned.

Phoebe glanced over at her sister. "It means someone wants to do harm to another."

Sophia looked up at Lord Mountgarret in confusion. "You wanted to hurt her grace? Why?"

"I didn't want to hurt my cousin," he defended.

"Then why would he say that?" Sophia asked.

Emeline smiled at the turn of the conversation as she trailed behind them.

"I didn't want to hurt my cousin, but a bad man did abduct her," Lord Mountgarret shared.

"Was it a Frenchman?" Phoebe asked. "His grace told me that all Frenchmen are the enemy."

He chuckled. "No. It wasn't a Frenchman. It was an acquaintance of Penelope's."

"Why would someone want to abduct her? She's so nice," Sophia pressed.

Lord Mountgarret nodded as he led them down the stairs. "That she is, but the man was trying to force her into a marriage."

"That wasn't nice of him," Phoebe declared.

"No, it wasn't."

Phoebe turned her gaze towards Lord Mountgarret. "How did his grace stop the bad man?"

"Why do you assume that his grace stopped him?"

"Did he?"

Lord Mountgarret entered the dining room and stood at the head of the table. Once they were situated, Lord Mountgarret took a seat and continued, "His grace was there, but I was the one who stopped the bad man."

"You were?" Sophia asked with a scrunched nose.

Lord Mountgarret smiled. "Well, it was more of a team

effort." As the first course was being served, he turned to Phoebe and asked, "Do you know how to ride?"

She nodded. "My father taught me."

"Excellent," he replied. "I have a calm horse I think would suit your needs. Would you care to take riding lessons?"

Phoebe stared at him in surprise. "I would, very much."

"Then so be it," he said with a smile.

"My father and I used to take rides around our estate every morning," Phoebe shared, reaching for her fork. "It was my favorite time of the day."

"Thank you for sharing that," Lord Mountgarret remarked. "I am not sure if you realized it, but your father and I were friends."

"I didn't know that," Phoebe replied.

"We attended Eton College and Oxford together. We studied to be barristers. During our holidays, we used to take long rides and tour the ruins on his father's property." Lord Mountgarret pressed his lips together and appeared to be blinking back tears. "I miss your father. He was a good man."

"He was," Phoebe murmured.

A silence descended over them.

After a few moments, Emeline asked, "Did your mother ride as well?"

Sophia nodded. "She loved riding. Sometimes Father would get angry at her because she would ride too fast."

"It's true," Phoebe confirmed. "I even saw her horse jump the hedges on more than one occasion."

"I think I would have liked your mother very much," Emeline said.

Phoebe smiled from across the table. "She would have liked you, as well."

"I'm afraid I didn't know your mother as well as your father," Lord Mountgarret started. "What was she like?"

"I remember Mother loved reading. She would always read to us after supper."

"She was kind," Sophia said, growing quiet.

"In what way?" Lord Mountgarret prodded.

"She would always check on me when it was thundering outside," Sophia shared.

"Are you afraid of thunder?" Emeline asked.

Sophia nodded. "I am."

Reaching over, Emeline placed her hand over Sophia's. "You can always come to me when you are scared, especially when it is thundering."

"You promise?"

She squeezed her hand. "I promise."

"Do you promise never to leave us?" Sophia asked softly.

Reluctantly, she admitted, "I'm afraid I can't make that promise."

"Why not?" Phoebe asked in a surprised tone.

"I intend only to stay on as your governess until either a new governess is secured or my twenty-first birthday, whichever is first."

Lord Mountgarret drew his dark brows together. "I beg your pardon?"

She turned towards him to explain. "This was never supposed to be a permanent position for me. I was hired by Mrs. Garvey only until she could find a new governess."

"You are leaving us?" Sophia asked.

"No, not for two months."

"Two months," Lord Mountgarret growled.

"I can't believe you are going to leave us, Miss Wren!" Phoebe shouted, tossing her napkin onto the table. She rose from her chair. "I hate you!"

She winced at Phoebe's harsh words. "You don't mean that, dear," she attempted, but Phoebe ran out of the room.

Sophia slipped her hand out from under hers. "Why are you leaving? Don't you like us anymore?"

"I do, very much so, but I'm afraid I am unable to stay," she said.

Sophia pushed back her chair. "You aren't supposed to leave, Miss Wren," she cried as she ran from the room.

Turning her gaze towards Lord Mountgarret, she saw that his jaw was clenched so tight that a muscled pulsated under his right ear.

"You're leaving?" he asked in a low tone.

She nodded sadly, feeling a bit guilty now. "Mrs. Garvey posted a notice in the newspaper a few days ago to advertise for the governess position."

"Are you unhappy here, Miss Wren?"

"I assure you that I am not."

"Then why would you leave?" he huffed. "Did you find a better opportunity?"

She shook her head. "I don't intend to seek other employment after I leave Rumney Manor."

"Explain to me why you would leave the girls?"

Lowering her gaze to the table, she replied, "I'm afraid I can't give you the answer you're seeking, my lord."

He shoved his chair back and tossed his napkin onto the plate. "I'm afraid I've lost my appetite, Miss Wren." He rose. "Will you at least stay until a new governess is hired on?"

"I can agree to that."

"Good."

"Lord Mountgarret..."

He spoke over her. "Good night, Miss Wren," he barked as he stormed out of the room, slamming the door behind him.

Picking up her fork, Emeline started moving her food idly around her plate. That went horribly, she thought. But to be fair, there was no easy way to tell them the truth. At least it was out in the open now.

Dropping her fork, she rose from her chair. Apparently, her appetite had left her, as well.

10

As the sun was just coming up over the horizon, Baldwin stood next to his mother's headstone. How he missed her! He missed her smile, her kindness, and more importantly, her advice.

How he wished he could ask his mother what he should do with his wards. Should he give up guardianship of them to their relatives or continue to raise them? Wouldn't it be better if they were raised by family rather than a complete stranger? Although, he believed he was making some progress with them. Phoebe had actually smiled at him last night over dinner.

Regardless, he had no idea how to rear children, and the one person who was navigating him through these unchartered waters was leaving. Miss Wren. An exasperating person who had managed to penetrate all his thoughts. How could he raise Phoebe and Sophia without her? No other governess would measure up to her. How could they? Miss Wren was kind, compassionate and had a brilliant smile that seemed to brighten up any room. But she was leaving them… leaving him.

Baldwin couldn't very well travel back to London today, not with Miss Wren's unsettling announcement. He felt compelled to stay at Rumney Manor, but he wasn't exactly sure why. Was it to spend more time with his wards or Miss Wren?

A horse whinnied in the distance, and he turned his head to see Miss Wren cresting the hill on her grey gelding. She was watching the sunrise with a look of deep contemplation on her face. With her blue riding habit, and her hair arranged into a low bun at the base of her neck, she was the picture of perfection. He took a moment to admire her riding posture and how at ease she looked on a horse.

It was evident she'd been born a lady. But what caused her to accept employment when she hadn't been seeking it? Her father was still alive. Why wasn't he providing for her? Why did she plan to leave on her twenty-first birthday? Was she in some type of danger? He had so many questions, but Miss Wren had not been forthcoming with her answers.

He saw the moment that Miss Wren recognized him, and he thought he saw a flicker of sadness cross her features. He raised his hand to greet her, and she slowly urged her horse towards him. His breath hitched in anticipation as she approached. That's an odd reaction, he thought to himself.

She stopped her horse a few yards from him, and her eyes darted towards his mother's headstone. "I apologize for intruding..."

"You aren't," he said, speaking over her. "Please join me."

After a small hesitation, she nodded. He watched as she gracefully slid off her horse and held the reins loosely in her hands.

She gave him a brief smile. "I see you are an early riser, my lord."

"I am, as are you."

With a wince, she shared, "That is true, but I must admit that I had a rough night last night, and I found myself wide awake before dawn."

"Did Sophia have another nightmare?"

"No," she murmured. "I spent most of the night assuring the girls that I wouldn't leave until another governess was found."

"I see."

She drew a deliberate, slow breath. "I would like to apologize..."

"There is no need, Miss Wren. You did nothing wrong."

"But I feel as though I did."

He fixed his gaze on her. "It is *I* that should apologize to you. I should never have left you alone at the dinner table."

"That's all right. I found that I wasn't particularly hungry myself."

His gaze shifted back towards his mother's headstone. "As I mentioned before, whenever I'm at Rumney Manor, I visit my mother's headstone every morning."

"I think that's admirable," she replied. "I often visit my mother's grave."

"Do you think Phoebe and Sophia would be better off being raised by family?" he asked, trying to shift the conversation away from himself.

"I thought they had no other family to speak of."

"What if they did?"

She considered him for a moment. "No," she said finally, "I do not think they would be better off. I think you're doing an admirable job."

He huffed. "I believe you need spectacles, then."

"There's a reason Mr. Barrington assigned you as his children's guardian," she started. "He trusted you to do right by them. To include them and to love them."

"But what if I fail?"

"To err on the side of love is seldom wrong," she counseled. "Just love them, my lord. Love them and cherish them."

He shifted his gaze towards the horizon. "Phoebe still hates me."

"Phoebe doesn't hate you, particularly after dinner last night. She was pleased that you offered her riding lessons."

"That's encouraging," he admitted.

"Just be your charming self, and it will all work out."

He brought his gaze to meet hers. "You think I'm charming?"

A blush came to her cheeks. "I... uh... *no*."

Taking pity on her, he turned his gaze back towards his mother's headstone, despite feeling pleased by her apparently positive opinion of him. "After Penelope's parents died, the Duke of Blackbourne became her guardian."

"Not your mother?"

He shook his head. "No. My mother even petitioned Parliament for custody, claiming her brother's will was outdated, but she was rejected."

"Did they state why?"

"The Duke of Blackbourne successfully argued that my father would take advantage of Penelope's wealth as her guardian, especially since he had already gambled away his family's fortune."

"That must have been hard on your mother."

He nodded. "It was. My parents had been estranged for years, so she felt the court's reasoning was flawed. The only time my mother saw my father was when he would parade his mistress around at any social gathering that they were both attending."

"How awful."

"Before my uncle's death, he paid for my education and assisted me when I applied to the Inns of Court. However, none of the established barristers would allow me to eat dinner with them because of my father's despicable reputation."

"They wouldn't let you eat dinner with them?" she asked in surprise.

He gave her an understanding smile. "These dinners were

actually meetings which included lectures or mock court sessions."

"Oh, I hadn't realized."

"Typically, at the end of three to five years, the senior members of the Inn of Courts would determine who would go on to be called to the bar. But the senior members told me that I would never be called." He hung his head. "I dropped out of the Inn of Courts after only two lonely months."

She took a step closer. "I am so sorry."

He turned to face her. "I decided then that I would focus on politics. I became an active member of the Tory party, spending all my time at the House of Lords, carefully avoiding any vices that were generally associated with gentlemen of the *ton*."

He chuckled dryly. "Since I was heavily in debt, I couldn't really afford most entertainment, much less my apartment at Albany. I didn't even employ a valet."

Growing sober, he admitted, "Furthermore, in order to change my circumstances, I knew I needed to marry a woman with a large dowry. I had come to terms that I was destined for a marriage of convenience, but that all changed when Penelope and Nicholas paid off my debts."

"How wonderful that you have such a kind cousin!"

"It is," he admitted, placing his hand on his mother's headstone, "but no matter how hard I work, no matter how much I accomplish, no one will let me forget my father's reputation. It has haunted me since the day I was born."

"You can rise above it," she said naively.

"I can't. The members of the House of Lords told me that I will never be elected Prime Minister because of my father's deplorable reputation. All my work has been wasted... again." He shook his head. "It's as if everyone is waiting for me to fail, to become like my father. And no matter how hard I try, I can't escape it. I can't forget him."

"You should never forget your father," she stated. "It's

because of him that you are the man you are today. Honest and forthright. A man of honor."

"Do you know what it's like for everyone to expect you to fail?"

She shook her head.

"It's exhausting," he answered, his shoulders slumping.

Miss Wren stepped forward and placed her hand over his. "You can prove the naysayers wrong."

He huffed. "I doubt it. Besides, I work in trade now."

"So?"

"A gentleman doesn't work for his income."

"That is utter nonsense."

He gave her a baffled look. "Doesn't it bother you that I work in trade?"

"Why would it?" she asked in such a way that he knew she was in earnest.

He looked down at her hand covering his, and for the first time, he didn't feel alone.

"You are unlike any woman that I have ever known before," he found himself admitting. With his other hand, he reached for her reins and secured them to a tree. "Come, I want to show you something."

As he held her gloved hand, he led her onto a small worn path through the trees, and they were immediately cloaked in green shade. The birds chirped merrily above them, squirrels scurried up the trees as they passed, and a deer froze in its place. He didn't stop until they reached a large pond with lily pads dotting the surface.

Without releasing her hand, he shared, "On the other side of the pond is Penelope's property."

"It's lovely here," Miss Wren said with a small sigh, her eyes scanning the trees.

His eyes remained fixated on her. "I agree completely."

A bullfrog croaked next to him, drawing her attention. "I

could spend hours here."

"Before Nicholas came to prepare Penelope for the Season, we used to meet in this spot," he shared.

A smile came to her face as she turned towards him. "Thank you for showing this to me."

"I thought you might enjoy it," he said, his eyes roaming her face.

Before she could respond, he heard a familiar voice from the other side of the pond. "Good morning, cousin. Miss Wren."

Miss Wren snatched her hand away and covered her flushed cheeks with her fingers. "Morning, your grace."

"Your grace?" Penelope asked with an arched eyebrow. "Since when do friends make use of titles when they're alone."

With a nervous laugh, Miss Wren started walking backwards. "My apologies. But… uh… I should be heading back to the nursery. The girls will be waking up soon."

"Wait," he urged, "allow me to escort you home."

"That isn't necessary, Lord Mountgarret. Please, stay and enjoy yourself," she said in a rush, obviously avoiding his gaze.

Baldwin watched as Miss Wren disappeared into the cover of the trees, then turned to face Penelope, who had a knowing look on her face.

"Emeline would make an excellent choice for a viscountess."

Ignoring her comment, Baldwin asked, "Where's Nicholas?"

She glanced over her shoulder. "Somewhere behind me. He was complaining about how I was going to break my neck if I continued racing so fast through the fields."

"I must concur with Nicholas. You are with child, after all."

"Just because I'm having a baby, doesn't mean I can't have fun anymore," she contended.

He shook his head. "I see becoming a duchess hasn't changed you at all."

She grinned. "Are you still bringing the girls by after breakfast to tour the shell grotto?"

"I am." He took a step backwards. "I shall see you in a few hours."

Penelope adjusted the reins in her hand. "Until then," she said, turning her horse around and racing it back down on the path she came from.

Walking along the worn path, Baldwin knew he'd better be careful, or his feelings for Miss Wren might deepen. And that should never happen while she was under his employ.

As the coach rolled away from Rumney Manor, Phoebe asked, "Do you think his grace will let us practice sword fighting today?"

Lord Mountgarret smiled over at her. "I don't see why not. After all, you are a part of his crew now."

Glancing out the window, Phoebe asked, "How many people do you think his grace has killed?"

"I would say at least a hundred Frenchmen," Sophia answered.

Phoebe shook her head. "No, I would say thousands."

"You're probably right," Sophia replied with a knowing nod.

Emeline gave Phoebe a disapproving shake of her head, causing her brown curls to sway back and forth. "Ladies do not speak of such things. You need to be mindful to engage only in polite conversation."

Phoebe frowned. "But I don't want to comment about the weather."

"It is vital that you develop the art of pleasing and polite exchange," Lord Mountgarret informed her.

"That sounds boring," Phoebe pouted.

Emeline grinned. "I must admit that it is rather annoying to hide your intellect when mingling with members of Society."

"Miss Wren..." Lord Mountgarret warned in a low tone.

Ignoring him, she said, "But you must think of it as a game."

"A game?"

She nodded. "A fun game."

"It doesn't sound very fun to me," Sophia stated.

"Many gentlemen of the *ton* don't want to associate with young women that are an intellectual threat to them. Furthermore, young ladies must be able to follow conversation, keep that conversation away from unpleasantries, and never be quick to offer advice," she explained.

"What is fun about that?" Phoebe asked.

Straightening her shoulders, she explained. "Every time I go out into Society, I know what's expected of me, and I behave properly. I discuss the weather, comment on the lovely gardens, and even converse about my embroidery skills." A playful smile came to her lips. "But I can still have fun."

"How?"

"I count how many crumbs can get stuck in a man's mustache, or how many times the matron will talk about herself, or I watch the debutantes as they flutter their eyelashes at the gentlemen," she said.

"That still doesn't sound like fun," Phoebe lamented.

"Life is about finding joy in the most mundane tasks," Miss Wren asserted. "We are all expected to behave in certain ways, to be someone that we aren't usually, but that doesn't mean we can't have fun on the journey."

Before anyone had a chance to respond, the coach came to a stop outside of a massive four-level medieval castle.

Both girls stared out the window in amazement.

"The duke and duchess live here?" Phoebe murmured.

"This castle is like out of a fairytale," Sophia said as a footman opened the coach door.

Once they had all stepped out of the coach, the main door to

Brighton Hall opened, and the duke and duchess descended the stairs.

Penelope wore a bright smile on her face. "Welcome to Brighton Hall. I'm so glad you've come."

Unexpectedly, both girls ran up to his grace and threw their arms around him. At first, the duke stood stiff, but then he relaxed and returned their embrace.

Phoebe looked up at him. "Can you tell us about your battles?"

"Phoebe..." Lord Mountgarret said in a warning tone.

"It's all right, Baldwin." His grace glanced down at the girls. "I would be happy to."

Penelope wore a look of amusement on her features. "Nicholas can go on and on about his naval victories. I fear that there may be too many to count."

"A captain always remembers his victories, my dear," Nicholas bragged.

Clasping her hands in front of her, Penelope asked, "Would you like to tour the underground grotto now?"

"Yes!" the girls shouted in unison.

"Follow me, then," Penelope said as she stepped down onto the paved courtyard. "It's around back in the gardens."

Lord Mountgarret offered his arm to her as the girls reached over to hold the duke's hands.

Speaking over her shoulder, Penelope shared, "It's the perfect time to visit the grotto because it is relatively dry now. When the river is high, it will drain into the grotto, making it nearly impossible to go in."

As they headed towards the rear of the estate, beautiful, well-maintained, gardens came into view, and a row of sculpted shrubs lined the footpath. In the center of the gardens, a spectacular cascade of water tumbled down stone steps in the hillside towards a large pond. Dabbling ducks swam complacently along the water's surface, occasionally sticking their heads into the water in their search for food.

The girls ran to the water's edge and crouched down. They put their hands out, attempting to pet the ducks.

His grace came to stand next to them. "Don't get too close, or you'll fall in," he warned.

"Can we pet the ducks?" Sophia asked.

The duke chuckled. "I don't think the ducks want to be petted."

"Can you swim, your grace?" Phoebe inquired, her eyes scanning the water.

"Every good sailor knows how to swim," he answered. "Don't you?"

Phoebe blew out a puff of air. "I don't."

"Then we shall have to teach you," he told her. "After all, every member of my crew must know how to swim."

"Can I learn, too?" Sophia asked.

The duke considered her for a moment before saying, "I don't know. You have to be at least eight to learn how to swim."

A bright smile came to her lips. "I am eight years old."

"Then I suppose I shall teach you, as well," his grace confirmed.

"We are almost to the grotto!" Penelope exclaimed in an excited voice as she started walking towards a small stone structure sitting back from the pond.

Penelope walked up to the building and opened the door. She spun back around. "This is the entrance. I urge you to be cautious as you walk down the stairs. The ground can be slippery. After the stairs, you will come to a long passageway that will eventually lead you to a rotunda." She placed her hand on the stone wall. "The walls along the corridor are covered with seashells."

"Follow me," Penelope said with a wave of her hand as his grace and the girls followed closely behind.

Lord Mountgarret dropped his arm and gestured towards the stone structure. "After you, Miss Wren."

"Thank you," she replied as she stepped into the darkened entry. She placed her hand on a banister running down the length of the stairs.

As she stepped into the passageway, Lord Mountgarret was by her side. Sconces hung on the walls, and the fishy odor of burning whale oil penetrated the small corridor.

"This is beautiful," she murmured as she ran her hands along the walls, which were covered with thousands of white seashells.

Lord Mountgarret's eyes scanned the walls. "It is."

Lowering her hand, she walked down the passageway. "His grace is wonderful with Phoebe and Sophia."

"I agree."

"Was the duke raised with a large family?"

He shook his head. "Not at all. He had an older brother who was killed in a tragic accident."

"How awful."

"It truly was. Unfortunately, many people still speculate that it wasn't an accident."

"In what way?"

"They believe Nicholas killed his brother to become the heir."

She glanced over at him with a shocked expression on her face. "They actually think his grace killed his own brother?"

"It's not true, of course, but the story adds to the allure of Nicholas, the Duke of Blackbourne. Not only is he a decorated captain, but he is also dangerous."

"He doesn't appear dangerous to me."

Lord Mountgarret chuckled. "Trust me, Nicholas can be quite intimidating when the situation calls for it."

Focusing on the seashells, Emeline wasn't watching where she was going and she stepped into a puddle of water, drenching her kid boots. "Fiddlesticks," she murmured.

"Watch your language, Miss Wren," Lord Mountgarret chided in a teasing tone.

"My boots are wet now."

He stopped. "Would you like me to carry you to the rotunda?"

"That's not necessary. I shall make do."

Clasping his hands behind his back, Lord Mountgarret said, "I appreciated your comments about finding joy in the mundane tasks."

"I must admit that it can be rather exhausting to be a young lady," she stated. "We are judged on the way we look, the way we compose ourselves, the way we speak, the way we play instruments, and the way we navigate through polite conversation."

"I had never considered that."

"Men are praised for their intelligence, but women who show any sort of prowess for learning are labeled as bluestockings," she continued, "and no man of sense would want a bluestocking for a wife."

He stopped. "That's not entirely true. I would rather have a woman who freely expresses her opinions than a silly woman who doesn't have any common sense."

"You are in the minority then, my lord."

They continued walking in comfortable silence until Lord Mountgarret spoke up. "I feel as though I know very little about you."

"What do you wish to know?"

"Let's start with an easy question." He kicked at a small pebble on the ground. "What is your favorite dessert?"

"Lemon cheesecake."

With a side-glance, he asked, "What is your favorite pastime?"

"That's a tie," she admitted. "I love riding, but there is nothing better than curling up on the settee with a good book."

"So, you're a bluestocking," he said, his tone teasing.

"I am," she admitted proudly.

Keeping his eyes straight ahead, he asked, "What is your greatest wish?"

"That's easy," she murmured. "I would like to see my mother one more time, to give her a hug and tell her that I love her."

"I feel the same way."

Her foot slipped on the wet ground, and Lord Mountgarret reached out, catching her elbow, holding her tightly. The impropriety of it was gone, queerly, as he turned her to face him.

"Careful, Miss Wren," he said in a hoarse voice.

She stared at him for a moment, transfixed. "Thank you for catching me."

Even in the dimly lit passageway, she could see his eyes darting towards her lips, and she waited with bated breath for him to say something, do anything. Her heart began to beat even faster, something she hadn't thought possible.

"Emeline..." he whispered as he came closer.

He watched her intently as he lowered his head, giving her ample time to protest if she so desired, which she had no intention of doing. Then, he kissed her. His kiss was soft, gentle and... perfect.

He leaned back a little, and his warm breath brushed over her lips as he said, "Forgive me, Miss Wren. I believe I got carried away."

"You are forgiven," she said in a breathless tone.

One of the girl's squealed with laughter down the hall, causing the spell to be broken. Lord Mountgarret dropped his hand from her elbow and took a step back.

"Shall we join them?" he asked, gesturing down the passageway.

She smiled coyly. "I think that's a brilliant idea, my lord."

Lord Mountgarret stiffened. "Perhaps it would be best if you went first, and I caught up to you."

Pressing her lips together, she asked, "Why?"

"I just need a moment alone, Miss Wren," he said abruptly.

"Of course," she said. "Take all the time you need."

As Emeline hurried down the long corridor, she found herself baffled by what had just transpired. Lord Mountgarret had kissed her! He'd kissed her, but then he'd dismissed her so easily. Had she done something wrong? She had never kissed anyone before. Perhaps her kiss repulsed him?

She truly hoped not. She wouldn't mind kissing the very handsome Lord Mountgarret again. Maybe, just maybe, he cared for her, too!

11

BALDWIN'S GAZE WAS FOCUSED OUT THE WINDOW AS HE SAT next to Phoebe in the carriage. They had just spent the afternoon at Brighton Hall and now were traveling back to his estate. His home. A place where he could finally be alone with his thoughts. He stifled a groan. What had he been thinking when he kissed Miss Wren? It was a moment of weakness. A moment that he immediately regretted. If anyone caught wind that he was dabbling with the governess, then everyone's opinion would be validated, that he was just like his father, an unscrupulous man who treated women deplorably. He refused to bring shame like that to Miss Wren. She was too sweet, too innocent.

His eyes darted towards Miss Wren. She was smiling at something Sophia had said, but he noticed the smile didn't reach her eyes. She almost appeared sad. Did he cause that?

After he'd kissed her, he'd gone out of his way to avoid her. He lingered back and avoided making eye contact with her. Whenever she glanced his way, Baldwin could see the questions lingering in her eyes.

Phoebe's excited voice drew his attention. "His grace told us about a battle where he was injured, and he still fought off a hundred French soldiers."

"That's true. He's a hero," Sophia stated.

"I would agree," Miss Wren said. "Any person who is protecting our King and country is a hero."

Glancing over at him, Sophia asked, "Why didn't you serve in the Navy?"

Baldwin gave her a tentative smile. "Sadly, I was not afforded the opportunity. Instead, I trained as a barrister."

"What's a barrister?" Sophia questioned.

Phoebe looked at her sister, took a deep breath, then recited, "Barristers are lawyers, and they present cases to the judges. Whereas solicitors deal with the more mundane matters which are beneath the notice of the barristers."

"Well said," he replied. "Where did you learn that?"

Phoebe gave him a smug look. "My father was a barrister, so he explained the difference to me in great detail."

"Your father was a very good barrister," he commented. "One of the best, perhaps."

Phoebe lowered her gaze. "I miss my parents."

He placed his arm around her shoulder to comfort her. "That's normal. A part of you will always miss them."

To his surprise, Phoebe leaned into him and rested her head against his chest.

He brought his gaze up and met Miss Wren's. She gave him an encouraging smile, and he found himself returning it. Perhaps he was finally breaking down Phoebe's barriers.

"Whose coach is that?" Sophia asked, pointing out the window.

Turning his gaze towards the window, he saw an unfamiliar black coach in front of Rumney Manor. Whoever could that be? He wasn't expecting any guests at this time.

Their coach came to a stop on the graveled courtyard, and a

footman opened the door. He waited until the girls and Miss Wren had exited the coach before he stepped down.

As he approached the main entrance, Mr. Drake held open the door and informed him, "Mr. Baker and Mr. and Mrs. Stewart are in your study, milord."

His steps faltered. "They are?"

"They claimed they had an appointment with you."

"Ah, yes," he replied. "Thank you."

"Very good, milord," Mr. Drake replied with a tip of his head.

Baldwin watched as Miss Wren escorted the girls up the stairs, wishing things could be different between them. No matter how deep his feelings ran for her, he couldn't dishonor her by bringing scandal to her name. She deserved better.

At the top of the stairs, she turned and met his gaze. He saw anguish in her eyes. Anguish that he'd caused. Rather than rush up the stairs to apologize, he tipped his head and proceeded towards his study. It was better this way. The kiss had been a mistake. A wonderful, terrible mistake.

As he stepped into his study, he saw Thomas's portly solicitor standing near the window.

"Welcome, Mr. Baker," he greeted. "I hadn't expected you to arrive so soon."

Mr. Baker turned to face him. "We made excellent time, milord." He gestured towards a young couple who had risen when he entered. "Lord Mountgarret, it is my pleasure to introduce you to Mr. and Mrs. Stewart." He smiled proudly. "Mrs. Stewart was Mr. Barrington's cousin."

Baldwin took a moment to assess the young, nicely dressed couple. Mr. Stewart was tall, with brown hair, broad shoulders, and a friendly air about him. His wife had brown hair, which was neatly coiffed, a slender nose, and an oval face.

Mr. Stewart tipped his head. "It's a pleasure to meet you, Lord Mountgarret."

"Likewise." He came around to sit behind his desk.

Mr. Baker shifted his gaze towards the Stewarts. "Mr. and Mrs. Stewart were hoping to collect the children, then we'll be on our way."

"I beg your pardon?" Baldwin asked in an irritated tone. "You expect me to release my wards to complete strangers?"

Mr. Baker looked unsure. "Forgive me, but I thought that was your intention."

"I have not made my decision yet."

Tightening her shawl around her arms, Mrs. Stewart stepped closer to the desk. "I understand your hesitancy, my lord. And I respect you more because of it. But perhaps if you get to know us, you will recognize that we will provide a good home for Miss Phoebe and Miss Sophia."

He pressed his lips tightly together in response.

With a side glance at her husband, Mrs. Stewart said, "We've been trying for nearly eight years to have children, but to no avail. We had almost given up hope that we would ever have children in our home when we discovered that my dear cousin, Thomas Barrington, had perished alongside his wife in that tragic accident."

Mr. Stewart stepped up next to his wife. "We made inquiries about what happened to the girls, which led us to Mr. Baker. He made it seem that you would be willing to grant us guardianship over the girls."

"That was my original intent, yes, but circumstances have changed," Baldwin said flatly.

"Surely, you must recognize that it would be better for the girls to be raised by family than by a bachelor, such as yourself," Mr. Stewart maintained.

Baldwin tapped the ledger on his desk with his finger. "That thought may have crossed my mind."

Mr. Baker spoke up. "The Stewarts have traveled all the way from London to meet with you."

"That *is* no small feat in a coach," Baldwin admitted.

Mr. Stewart's eyes roamed his study. "Our small estate in Worchester is not nearly as lavish as your estate, my lord, but we do employ a few servants, and the girls would want for nothing."

"Does your estate bring in an income, Mr. Stewart?" he asked.

Mr. Stewart nodded. "It does. We own a large pig farm, and we produce enough income to meet our needs."

"How much is that exactly?" he questioned.

"About £100 pounds annually."

Baldwin considered them for a moment before inquiring, "Has Mr. Baker informed you that the girls have inherited their father's estate?"

"Yes, he did mention that, vaguely, but that's not why we're here," Mr. Stewart asserted.

"Need I remind you that Miss Phoebe and Miss Sophia are heiresses," Baldwin stated. "*If* I did turn over guardianship to you, I would retain the position as the testamentary guardian, which means I will be responsible for delegating their allowance."

"That's to be expected," Mr. Stewart said.

Crossing his arms over his chest, he asked Mrs. Stewart, "Why do you suppose Thomas didn't list you as guardian?"

"I cannot even presume to guess," she murmured.

"Furthermore, I don't recall seeing you at Thomas's wedding, or either of his daughters' christenings," Baldwin continued.

Mr. Stewart touched his wife's arm. "It's all right. You can tell him the truth."

With a sad smile, Mrs. Stewart shared, "My father wasn't the best of men." Her breath hitched with emotion. "Because of his reputation, we were ostracized by my uncle and his family. I'm not proud of my father's past, but I've learned to acknowledge that it was my past, too. When I learned that Thomas had died," she paused, "I realized it was too late to make amends with him."

Mr. Stewart placed his arm over his wife's shoulder. "Which is why raising the girls is so important to us. We feel as though we owe it to Thomas to raise his children with love and kindness. Just as he would."

Baldwin uncrossed his arms and brought them to his side. "I understand what you went through, Mrs. Stewart. My father also had a deplorable reputation. One that still follows me to this day."

She nodded her understanding. "If you grant us the privilege of raising Phoebe and Sophia, I promise you won't regret it."

"I must adjourn and consider this matter carefully," Baldwin stated.

"Of course," Mr. Stewart agreed. "You can reach us at the public house in town."

"Nonsense. You shall stay here as my guests. Furthermore, that will give you the chance to meet the girls, and they can get to know you."

A bright smile came to Mrs. Stewart's lips. "How delightful."

"If you will excuse me, I shall inform my housekeeper to prepare rooms for you. The dinner bell will chime shortly."

"Thank you for your hospitality, Lord Mountgarret," Mr. Stewart said.

He bowed and exited the room in search of his housekeeper. He had no idea what to think about Mr. and Mrs. Stewart, only that their presence troubled him greatly.

Emeline had just finished coiffing Phoebe's hair when the girl asked, "Why do we have to wear our nice dresses for dinner?"

"I already told you that Lord Mountgarret has guests for dinner," she answered.

"Can't we just eat dinner in the nursery, then?" Sophia asked hopefully.

She shook her head. "No, Lord Mountgarret specifically requested your presence this evening. Which means you must be on your best behavior." She gave Phoebe a pointed look. "Remember, only polite conversation topics."

Phoebe dropped down onto the chair. "This dinner is going to be dreadfully boring."

"I agree," Sophia said.

Emeline took a moment to smooth back her hair. "Will you please just give Lord Mountgarret's guests a chance... *please*."

"Fine," Phoebe said, rising, "but I refuse to talk about the weather."

"But the weather has been so pleasant lately," Emeline teased as she walked over to the door. She held out her hands to the girls. "Come, Lord Mountgarret asked for us to gather in the drawing room before dinner."

The girls came and held her hands. A few moments later, they arrived at the drawing room to witness a heated exchange between a portly, blond-haired man and a beautiful woman. They were speaking in low tones near the fireplace, but they were glaring at each other with such intensity that it was palpable.

A tall gentleman quickly rose from a chair. "Evening," he said in a loud voice, causing the other members of the room to stop their discussion.

When the woman turned to face them, she had a smile on her face. "These two lovely girls must be Miss Phoebe and Miss Sophia."

Both Phoebe and Sophia stepped closer to her as Emeline replied, "You would be correct."

The woman approached them, stopping only when they were an arm's length apart. "It's a pleasure to meet you. My name is

Mrs. Bridget Stewart." She gestured over her shoulder at the tall gentleman. "And that is my husband, Mr. James Stewart."

Phoebe dropped into a slight curtsy, earning an approving nod from Mrs. Stewart.

"You must be Phoebe," the woman said.

Phoebe nodded. "Yes, ma'am."

Mrs. Stewart turned her gaze towards Sophia. "And you must be Sophia."

Sophia bobbed her head weakly.

Meeting Emeline's gaze, Mrs. Stewart remarked, "I assume you are the governess."

"I am."

"You are dismissed for the evening."

The girls looked up at her in a panic, and Sophia tightened her grip on Emeline's hand.

"With all due respect, Mrs. Stewart," she started, "I normally eat dinner with the girls and Lord Mountgarret."

Mrs. Stewart looked annoyed by her response. "I am surprised that Lord Mountgarret allows the help to eat dinner with him when he has invited guests to join him."

Recognizing the validity of her argument, she released Sophia's hand. "You have a valid point. I shall adjourn for the evening."

"But, Miss Wren..." Sophia's sweet voice protested.

Mrs. Stewart put her hand out to Sophia. "Come along, child. Your governess needs some time to herself."

Sophia stared at Mrs. Stewart's proffered hand before she tentatively reached out and accepted it. Mrs. Stewart then led her over to the settee.

Emeline remained motionless for a moment before she spun around and walked out into the entry hall. For some unknown reason, tears sprang to her eyes, and she quickly blinked them away. Why did it bother her that she wouldn't be having dinner with the girls and Lord Mountgarret this evening?

"May I ask where you are going, Miss Wren?" Lord Mountgarret asked as he walked down the stairs.

"To the library," she answered in a shaky voice.

He came to stop in front of her, and his eyes roamed her face. "You've been crying," he replied, his compassion evident in his voice.

"It was only a moment of weakness, my lord."

He glanced over her shoulder at the drawing room door. "Don't you intend to join us for dinner?"

"Mrs. Stewart has dismissed me for the evening."

"I beg your pardon?" he asked, his voice rising.

She smoothed out her ivory gown. "I assure you that it is quite all right. You have guests, and I would hate to intrude."

"Regardless, I would like you to join us for dinner. We had a deal, remember?"

"I do, but..."

Lord Mountgarret offered her his arm. "Please, join us."

She glanced down at his proffered arm for a moment before she made her decision. Placing her hand on his, she said, "Thank you, I believe I will."

He looked over and graced her with a dashing smile. "Besides, I asked the cook to prepare lemon cheesecake for dessert."

"You remembered."

"Of course, I remembered," he said lightly. "I remember everything you say." He then cleared his throat, almost as if he was embarrassed by that admission.

He escorted her into the drawing room, remaining by her side as he announced, "Miss Wren has graciously agreed to join us for dinner."

"How delightful," Mr. Stewart said as he rose from his chair.

In a hushed voice, he asked, "Have you been introduced to Mr. and Mrs. Stewart?"

"Not formally," she admitted quietly.

"Miss Wren, I would like to introduce you to Mr. and Mrs. Stewart," he said in a more normal tone, "and Mr. Baker."

The portly man stepped away from the fireplace and bowed. "It's a pleasure to meet you, Miss Wren."

She tipped her head graciously. "Likewise, Mr. Baker."

Rising from her seat on the settee, Mrs. Stewart had a strained smile on her face. "How delightful it will be to have another woman at the table this evening."

Sophia jumped up from the settee and ran over to her. "I'm so glad you are joining us for dinner, Miss Wren!"

At that moment, the butler stepped into the room and announced dinner was ready to be served. They adjourned to the formal dining room, where Lord Mountgarret claimed the head of the table, his guests on one side, and the girls and Emeline on the other.

As the first course was being served, Lord Mountgarret shared, "Mr. and Mrs. Stewart own a pig farm up north."

Sophia looked up in excitement. "Do you have baby pigs?"

"Yes, we had nearly a hundred piglets this spring," Mr. Stewart confirmed.

Phoebe joined the conversation by sharing, "Pigs have an exceptional sense of smell."

"I am very impressed that you know that, young lady," Mr. Stewart praised. "Because of their excellent smell, and their foraging abilities, we use a select group of pigs to hunt for truffles in the woodlands."

"Our country estate in Bath had a small pig farm next to the crops," Phoebe explained. "Sophia and I used to help feed them in the morning."

"Do you remember what you fed them?" Mr. Stewart inquired.

Phoebe nodded. "If I recall correctly, we fed them leaves, fruits, grass, roots, and flowers."

"Those were well fed pigs," Mr. Stewart said, smiling.

Sophia giggled. "It was fun to watch them dig in the mud."

Mr. Stewart chuckled. "I have never heard of anyone who enjoyed watching pigs, especially since their stench can be quite offensive."

Phoebe grew silent for a moment. "For some, the smell of pig manure might be disgusting, but it reminds me of home."

Lord Mountgarret spoke up from the head of the table. "Perhaps Rumney Manor needs a pig farm near the woodlands."

Phoebe's eyes grew wide. "Do you mean that?"

"We have more than enough space to contain a *small* pig farm, and it might be fun to see the little piglets running around," he added.

A wide smile came to the girl's lips. "Can I have a piglet as a pet?"

"Pigs are not pets, dear," Mrs. Stewart said. "Pigs are food."

Lord Mountgarret grinned. "I daresay a pig might be a better pet than a frog."

"Dear heavens, why would anyone want a frog for a pet?" Mrs. Stewart inquired haughtily.

"I agree, Mrs. Stewart," Lord Mountgarret replied as he winked at Phoebe.

Emeline smiled at the touching interaction between Lord Mountgarret and his ward. Just as she had predicted, eating dinner together was bringing them closer.

12

BALDWIN SLAMMED THE LEDGER CLOSED. HE HAD REREAD THE same line over and over, and he was getting nowhere with balancing the books. He needed to focus on the task at hand, but that was proving nearly impossible because his mind kept returning to the Stewarts. They were his wards' family and appeared to be a kind and loving couple.

They had the funds to raise Phoebe and Sophia, and he would ensure the girls received a generous monthly allowance. So, they would not want for anything. It seemed like an ideal fit, but he couldn't shake the feeling that it was the wrong choice. Was it for selfish purposes he now wanted to keep the girls, especially since he had finally broken through Phoebe's barriers? And would he feel differently once Miss Wren left?

Miss Wren.

He'd kissed her.

He couldn't seem to forget it, no matter how hard he tried. The kiss had meant something to him. It had awakened something deep inside of him, but he didn't know for certain what that was. For so long, he'd insisted that he didn't want a wife or a family. But what if he truly did? What if there was more to life than being a bachelor and running a company? He was tired of being lonely, and his wards had given him an escape from his life of loneliness.

"May I enter, milord?" his man of business asked from the doorway.

Baldwin waved him in. "Please, come in."

With a file in his hand, Henry walked further into the room and commented, "You seem out of sorts today."

"I am, but it's nothing to concern you with."

Henry stopped next to the chair in front of the desk. "Did you go riding this morning?"

"I did. In fact, I only just got back."

"Interesting," he murmured. "Generally speaking, you are usually much less cantankerous once you've had your morning ride."

Baldwin pursed his lips together. "Do you have a particular reason you're here, or is it just to annoy me?"

"Wouldn't it be enough that I just came to visit a friend?"

"No."

Opening the file, Henry extended it towards him. "I found some farmland I thought you would be interested in purchasing. It is just north of your property line and would add nearly fifty acres to your property."

"Buy it."

"I assumed as much, so I already negotiated a price on it." He pointed at a sheet of paper. "That was the agreed upon sum."

Baldwin nodded in approval. "That sounds reasonable."

"With your approval, I intend to inform the tenants that they may remain on the land, assuming they continue to farm it."

"Agreed."

Henry sat down. "Excellent. Is there anything else?"

"Actually, there is," he said. "I was wondering if you could hire a pig farmer."

Henry's brows shot up. "A pig farmer? May I ask why?"

"Last night, I was talking with Phoebe..."

"Who is Phoebe?"

"My ten-year-old ward."

"Ah, proceed."

"And she seemed keen on the idea of having a small pig farm on the east side of my property."

Henry stared at him with a bewildered look on his face. "You want a pig farm on your property... *willingly?*"

"Yes."

Rising, Henry leaned over the desk and looked at him in concern. "Are you feeling all right? Should I fetch the doctor?"

He tugged down on the lapels of his jacket. "I am perfectly well."

"Pigs reek."

"I am aware of that fact."

"And you are doing this on a whim for your ward?"

He rose from his chair and walked over to the window. "Her father had a pig farm on his land, and she mentioned the smell of pigs remind her of home."

"That's commendable, but I would proceed with caution. Pigs are a big commitment."

"I understand. Would you mind making some inquiries and interviewing the pig farmers?"

Henry stood up, closed the file on the desk, and picked it up. "Have you considered how many pigs you would like?"

"No more than ten."

Henry studied him with a look of amusement on his face. "What has transpired these past eight days?"

"Nothing out of the ordinary."

"No?" Henry questioned. "Last time we spoke, you wanted nothing to do with your wards, and now you are taking up pigs to make them happy."

Outside of his window, he saw Phoebe was sitting atop a gelding, receiving instructions from the lead groomsman in a gated pasture. A smiling Sophia was sitting on top of the fence, and Miss Wren was standing behind her.

"You're smiling," Henry said from next to him. "You hardly smile."

"I smile."

"Very rarely." Henry glanced out the window. "I'm curious as to what is causing your smile. Is it your wards, or the beautiful governess that you can't stop staring at?"

"I don't have dalliances with the help," Baldwin replied in a firm voice.

"Of course not, milord."

He turned to face his man of business. "I need your advice."

"Is it about how you tie your cravats?" Henry asked.

Glancing down at his cravat, he frowned. "What's wrong with my cravat?"

"The fact that you have to ask that question makes me sad for you."

He huffed. "That's not what I wanted to talk to you about."

"Is it about how you…"

"Enough," he declared, speaking over him. "I have something important I need to speak to you about."

"I'm listening," Henry said, growing serious.

Baldwin frowned. "Relatives of Phoebe and Sophia have been found."

"I thought they didn't have any immediate relations to speak of."

"Neither did I, but apparently Thomas's cousin approached Mr. Baker about the children."

"Who is Mr. Baker?"

"He was Thomas's solicitor, and the one who informed me about guardianship over the girls."

Henry bobbed his head. "What exactly is the problem?"

"The Stewarts have traveled from London in an attempt to gain guardianship over the girls."

"Do they reside in London?" Henry asked.

"No, they live in Worchester, but they went to London to speak to Mr. Baker."

Henry hmphed. "Do you want to give up being a guardian to your wards?"

"I don't know."

"You don't know?" Henry repeated incredulously. "Well, you'd better figure it out, and quickly."

Walking over to the settee, Baldwin dropped down onto it. "On one hand, I've grown to care for the girls and want them to remain as my wards. But I can't help but think it might be best for the girls to be raised by their family."

"Family isn't always blood," Henry said, walking closer. "I can't help but notice that you seem to have bonded with your wards. Why would you give up guardianship?"

He rested his head on the back of the camelback settee. "After my aunt and uncle died, my cousin, Penelope, became the ward of the Duke of Blackbourne. It broke my mother's heart that she'd been taken away from her family."

"Your cousin married the Duke of Blackbourne. I believe, in that situation, it was for the best."

"What kind of monster would I be if I kept the girls away from their family?"

Henry sighed as he came to sit next to him. "I recommend two things. First, you need to go speak to her grace about this."

"I think that would be for the best. And the second thing?"

"You grant me permission to investigate Mr. and Mrs. Stewart. They only live in Worchester, so I could travel there and back by tomorrow."

Furrowing his brow, he asked, "Do you doubt who they claim to be?"

"Not necessarily, but it's best to be cautious. After all, your wards are heiresses."

"That's an excellent point. It would be prudent to send you to

Worcester to ensure the Stewarts have a good reputation in their town."

Henry's eyes strayed over to the window. "Just a thought, but if you don't have wards, you won't have a need for the pretty governess."

"She's leaving anyway."

"She is?" Henry asked in surprise. "What did you do?"

"Nothing. She informed me that this position is only temporary, and once a new governess is found, she will be leaving."

"To a new employer?"

He shook his head. "She won't say."

"Interesting," Henry said slowly. "She is a woman of intrigue."

"Go away."

Rising from his seat, Henry announced, "I believe my work here is done."

"You didn't do anything."

"Ah, you're wrong. I suggested you go speak to her grace about your situation."

"That you did."

"As always, it has been a pleasure, milord." Henry bowed before departing.

Baldwin rose from his seat and stepped over to the mirror. He would go speak to Penelope and his grace as soon as he figured out what in the blazes was wrong with his cravat.

Emeline stood behind Sophia as she sat on the top rung of the fence enclosing a green pasture. They were watching Phoebe as the groomsman gave her a riding lesson.

"You must ensure that you are sitting securely in the middle, and your hips should be square to the horse," the groomsman instructed as Phoebe rode in a tight circle around him.

Phoebe had a bright smile on her face as she sat atop the horse.

Turning her gaze towards Rumney Manor, Emeline saw that Lord Mountgarret was watching them from his study window. Most likely, he was watching his wards, and not her. After he'd kissed her, Lord Mountgarret had gone out of his way to avoid being alone with her. He clearly regretted his actions, but she hadn't. She had found the kiss to be exceptionally wonderful.

It was fortunate she was leaving soon, because she doubted her heart could take his rejection much longer. For someone who prided herself on her sensibility, she felt more like a simpering female whenever she thought about the handsome lord.

She saw him move away from the window and turned her gaze back towards the pasture.

"Very good, Miss Phoebe," the groomsman said as he assisted her off the horse.

"May I come back tomorrow for further instruction?" Phoebe asked once her feet were on the ground.

Reaching for the reins, the groomsman replied, "I shall plan on it."

"Thank you." Phoebe ran over to the fence and asked in an excited voice, "Did you see me, Miss Wren?"

"I did."

Phoebe twirled in a circle. "That was so much fun."

Turning back to face her, Sophia asked, "Can I start riding lessons?"

"You'll have to ask Lord Mountgarret."

Sophia climbed down off the fence. "Let's go ask him now," she suggested eagerly, reaching for her hand.

"We could, or we could go into the woodlands and look for plants," Emeline countered.

Phoebe ducked between the rungs of the fence. "Can we dip our feet in the stream?"

"I don't see why not."

Both girls cheered.

Emeline gave them a warm smile. Phoebe and Sophia were such delightful girls, and they were so easy to please. They just wanted someone to give them attention and care for them. She was pleased that Lord Mountgarret had started recognizing that. His suggestions of riding lessons and putting a small pig farm on his property were wonderful.

After she tightened the strings on her simple hat, she crouched down and retied Sophia's bonnet.

"Let's go before it gets any hotter outside," she suggested as she rose.

"Morning, girls," Mrs. Stewart proclaimed in a cheery voice as she approached them.

Emeline took a moment to admire the pale pink gown with a square neckline that Mrs. Stewart wore, but she resisted the urge to giggle at the large, flowery, straw hat atop her head.

The girls did their best to hide their frowns as Mrs. Stewart stopped in front of them. They both mumbled, "Morning, Mrs. Stewart."

"May I join you on your walk?" Mrs. Stewart asked, glancing between them.

Both girls lowered their gazes, refusing to answer. Rather than take the hint, Mrs. Stewart brought her gaze up and inquired, "Where shall we walk to?"

Emeline spoke up. "We were planning on taking a stroll into the woodlands and look for plants that have medicinal purposes."

"What a clever approach to teaching botany," Mrs. Stewart remarked. "I believe I can help with this lesson."

"Are you familiar with botany?" she asked.

Mrs. Stewart gave her a condescending smile. "I was sent to

boarding school at a young age, and I was taught a wide range of subjects."

"Which boarding school did you attend?"

"I was sent to one in Witney," Mrs. Stewart stated dismissively.

Tired of the woman's condescending attitude, Emeline remarked, "I attended Miss Bell's Finishing School."

Mrs. Stewart gave her a puzzled look. "You attended Miss Bell's Finishing School?"

"I did," she answered proudly.

"Miss Bell's Finishing School is a most prestigious school," Mrs. Stewart commented. "Pray tell, how did you end up as a governess?"

Rather than look ashamed, Emeline met her gaze and replied, "It is a long, complicated story."

"I would like to hear it sometime," Mrs. Stewart said, but her tone belied her words, instead reflecting a complete lack of interest.

Holding her hands out, Emeline asked, "Shall we, girls?"

The girls quickly latched onto her, and they started walking towards the woodlands lining the property, not bothering to wait for Mrs. Stewart.

"Does Lord Mountgarret allow his wards to go into the woodlands without an escort?" Mrs. Stewart asked from behind them.

"I am escorting them," Emeline said over her shoulder.

"What about footmen?"

"They are not necessary."

"But what if you encounter wolves?" Mrs. Stewart questioned.

Tightening her hold on the girls' hands, she answered, "Do not fear. We have yet to see wolf tracks in these woodlands."

"What about snakes?"

Phoebe answered, "We have only seen snake skins, no live snakes yet."

Mrs. Stewart's steps faltered. "Dear heavens. You can't be serious about going into those woods, are you?"

"I am."

"What about wild boars?"

"Boars are more afraid of us than we are of them."

Mrs. Stewart muttered, "I doubt that."

Stopping at the woodland entrance where they normally walked, Emeline turned to face the skittish woman. "It might be best if you don't join us for the next leg of our journey. I'm afraid it might be a little too taxing for a woman such as yourself."

"Don't be ridiculous," Mrs. Stewart declared with a wave of her hand. "I'm excited for this little adventure."

"Suit yourself," Emeline replied as she turned onto a worn path between the birches.

As she led the girls deeper into the woodlands, a green canopy of leaves covered them as they walked past shrubbery and moss-coated tree trunks. The ground was covered with bluebells and wood anemones.

Stopping on the trail, Emeline crouched down and pointed to a plant with white flowers. "Can you tell me what this plant is?"

Phoebe proudly answered, "Garlic."

"Very good," she said, "and what medicinal purposes does garlic have?"

Sophia scrunched her nose, then said, "It helps ease stomach pain."

Rising, Emeline added, "Yes, the herb does help ease stomach pain. We also use it to flavor our butter."

The sound of a trickling stream in the distance reached Emeline's ears. "Come, we're almost there," she encouraged. "Keep your eye out for more plants."

As they approached the stream, Sophia stopped and pointed

at a section of bright orange colored flowers. "Those are marigolds."

"Well done, Sophia," Emeline praised as she ripped off a few petals. "What medicinal purposes do marigolds have?"

"They help with headaches and toothaches," Phoebe recited.

"That's right."

Emeline handed a petal to each of the girls before she placed one in her mouth, enjoying the citrus flavor.

Sophia ate the petal, and her eyes grew wide with pleasure. "Those are delicious. May I have another?"

"You may," she replied, pulling off another petal and extending it towards her. She turned her gaze towards Mrs. Stewart. "Would you like to try a marigold petal?"

She shook her head. "No, thank you."

"They are quite tasty," Phoebe shared as she helped herself to another petal.

Mrs. Stewart stiffened. "I shall pass."

"If you insist," Emeline said as she turned her attention towards the rocky stream.

The girls ran up next to the stream and sat down on a large boulder. They were in the process of taking off their boots and stockings when Mrs. Stewart asked, "What do you girls think you are doing?"

They froze and turned their questioning gaze towards Emeline.

"They're going to place their feet into the cool stream," she explained calmly.

Mrs. Stewart frowned. "That is unacceptable. It is never appropriate to have one's shoes off in public." She lowered her voice. "What if a man stumbled upon this?"

"I doubt that would happen, since we are still on Lord Mountgarret's land," Emeline countered.

A brown frog with dark blotches croaked near Phoebe's feet. Giggling, Phoebe reached down and picked up the frog with both hands. "What a beautiful frog you are." She held it up with pride. "Would you care to see it, Miss Wren?"

"I would," Emeline responded, walking closer to admire the frog.

Sophia reached out and touched the frog's head. "It's slimy."

A mischievous smile came to Phoebe's lips as she rose from the boulder and turned to face Mrs. Stewart. "Would you like to see the frog?"

Mrs. Stewart glanced at the frog with a look of disgust. "Absolutely not."

"Why not?" Phoebe asked.

Taking a step back, Mrs. Stewart said, "Get that disgusting thing away from me."

Phoebe took a step closer, holding it up to show it to her. "Are you sure?"

"I am." Mrs. Stewart took another step back and slipped on a rock, causing her to fall into the stream.

Mrs. Stewart rose, stepped out of the stream, and looked down at her drenched skirt. With a fiery look in her eyes, she glared at Phoebe. "Look at what you've done!"

Leaning down, Phoebe released the frog onto the ground. "I'm sorry. I didn't mean…"

Mrs. Stewart put her hand up and pressed her lips together. "If you will excuse me, I shall return to Rumney Manor to change." She dropped her hand. "I have no choice but to inform Lord Mountgarret of your horrid behavior."

With her head held high, Mrs. Stewart started back down on the path, her wet shoes making a squishing noise every time she took a step.

After Mrs. Stewart was out of view, Emeline gave Phoebe her sternest glare. "Do you want to tell me what that was all about?"

"I don't like her. She's mean," Phoebe replied with downcast eyes.

"Regardless, Mrs. Stewart is Lord Mountgarret's guest and should be treated with respect," she contended. "I expect you to apologize to her when we get back to the estate."

"But…" Phoebe huffed.

She spoke over her. "No, 'buts'. You will apologize to her."

Phoebe nodded her head in response.

"Good," Emeline said in an approving tone. "Now, I think it is time we dipped our feet into the stream."

"Do you mean that?" Sophia asked.

She smiled. "I do."

The girls squealed with excitement as they removed their stockings. She had no doubt Lord Mountgarret would chastise her and Phoebe, so she might as well enjoy the cool water on her toes.

13

EMELINE WATCHED AS LORD MOUNTGARRET PACED ACROSS HIS study with a scowl on his face. She reached over and patted Phoebe on the leg, hoping to provide much needed reassurance.

Lord Mountgarret stopped pacing and stared at Phoebe. "I want you to explain to me how Mrs. Stewart ended up in the stream," he said sternly.

Phoebe sat up in her seat. "I was attempting to show her a frog."

"A frog?" Lord Mountgarret repeated in dismay. "You were trying to show Mrs. Stewart a frog?"

She lowered her gaze to the carpet. "Yes, I thought she might like it."

"Did she?"

Phoebe shook her head. "No, my lord."

He shifted his gaze towards her. "Where were you when this happened?"

"I was standing next to the girls."

Lord Mountgarret's tone was both accusatory and incredulous. "May I ask why you insist on allowing Phoebe to play with frogs, Miss Wren?"

"There's no harm in it."

"Do I have to specifically make a rule stating that my wards are not allowed to play with reptiles?"

She tilted her chin stubbornly. "Frogs are not reptiles. Besides, did you not play with frogs when you were younger?"

"I did, but that's entirely different."

"Why is that?"

"I was a boy."

"And Phoebe is a girl, my lord."

Pursing his lips, he said, "Girls need to act with decorum and grace. They cannot be running around woodlands and playing with snakes."

"I was teaching them botany," Emeline insisted. "We were finding plants that have medicinal purposes, such as wild garlic and marigolds. Your woodlands have the perfect conditions for many of these herbs."

"I respect that young ladies need to understand botany, but as I have insisted before, you should teach them lessons from the many books that I have in the library."

"And, *again*, I must respectfully decline that suggestion. Children learn botany better when presented with live plants, not just pictures and descriptions."

Lord Mountgarret tossed back his head and heaved a deep sigh. "You are quite vexing, Miss Wren." He brought his gaze back down to meet hers. "Mrs. Stewart was furious after she returned from the woodlands. She even demanded that I fire you."

"That doesn't surprise me," Emeline muttered.

"Perhaps I'm mad for not firing you, especially since you are supposed to be teaching the girls how to behave like proper ladies."

Phoebe let out a gasp. "You can't fire Miss Wren. It was my fault that Mrs. Stewart fell into the water, not hers."

"Go to the nursery, Phoebe!" Lord Mountgarret shouted as he

pointed towards the door. "As your punishment, you shall go without supper tonight."

Emeline slipped her arm over Phoebe's shoulder and whispered, "It's all right."

Tears came to the girl's eyes. "He can't fire you."

"It will all work out," Emeline said, wiping away a tear rolling slowly down Phoebe's cheek. "I promise."

Phoebe bobbed her head and rose slowly. She turned to face Lord Mountgarret. "I am sorry for my actions today."

Lord Mountgarret crossed his arms over his chest. "Thank you for that, but you also owe Mrs. Stewart an apology as well."

"I know," Phoebe murmured softly.

"Now, off with you," he ordered in a firm tone. "Miss Wren will be up shortly."

Emeline watched as Phoebe walked out of the room and closed the door behind her. She turned her attention back towards Lord Mountgarret with an expectant look on her brow.

Lord Mountgarret watched her for a long moment before saying, "You are no longer allowed to go into the woodlands with the girls."

"I think you're being rather hasty."

"I am not," he declared. "It's not proper for a girl of Phoebe's age to play with frogs. I think her time would be better spent working on her penmanship or practicing on the pianoforte."

"Phoebe already spends over an hour a day practicing the pianoforte."

"Then make it two hours a day."

She paused. "Do you intend for me to take all the fun out of their lessons as well?" she asked dryly.

"Miss Wren…" he started in a warning tone.

She rose from her seat. "Every day, these girls spend the majority of their day inside working on lessons. Their education is not lacking in the slightest."

"Clearly it is, if you escape to the woodlands," he challenged.

She pressed her lips together. "Are the girls not allowed to take walks? Are they your prisoners?"

"No, they are not my prisoners," he replied in an exasperated tone.

"But you insist that they remain indoors all day."

"I never said that."

"You implied it." Crossing her arms over her chest, she asked, "Is it acceptable for the girls to look out the windows or should we board those up?"

He groaned. "You are an infuriating woman, Miss Wren."

"First, I was vexing, and now I am infuriating. Which one am I?"

He took a commanding step towards her. "You are both!" he shouted.

Lord Mountgarret was close enough that she had to tilt her head to look up at him. "The girls need to have some form of escape. Their walks help channel their excess energy," she argued.

Being this close to Lord Mountgarret, she couldn't help but admire his strong jawline, and even begrudgingly admitted to herself that he was even more attractive when his jaw was covered with a slight stubble.

She forced herself to meet his gaze, hoping he would see how determined she was. "I assure you that I am teaching these girls everything they need to know to be proper ladies. You must trust me."

"That's the point, Miss Wren," he said. "I don't trust you."

She took a step back. "Pardon?"

He sighed as he dropped his head. "It is not just you that I don't trust with my wards. I don't trust myself."

"Why? You are doing a wonderful job with the girls," she insisted.

"Am I?" he asked. "I just sent a ten-year-old off to bed with no supper because she played with a frog."

"Eight days ago, the girls thought you hated them. They could scarcely be in the same room with you," she shared. "But now, they freely engage with you and even smile at you. You are making remarkable progress."

His shoulders slumped. "For so long, I have only been concerned with my own wants and needs, I don't know how to raise children."

"The first thing you must understand is that every child is different. They all have different wants and expectations. For example, Phoebe is rebellious and adventurous, whereas Sophia just wants to please everyone."

"What am I going to do without you?"

She took a step closer to him. "You don't need me to raise these girls."

"Don't I?"

"You're stronger than you give yourself credit for."

He huffed. "You're wrong." He walked over to the drink cart as he shared, "The Stewarts aren't just my guests. They are cousins of the girls' father."

"They are?"

Taking the stopper off the decanter, he nodded. "They have come to persuade me to grant them guardianship of Phoebe and Sophia."

"You aren't going to give it to them, are you?" she asked, approaching him.

"I haven't decided yet."

She placed a hand on his sleeve. "You must believe me that Mrs. Stewart is not a good fit for the girls."

"Why, because she composes herself with decorum at all times?" he asked sarcastically.

She stared at him in disbelief as she withdrew her hand. "Why would you even be considering it?"

"Because, Miss Wren," he began, "it might be best if the girls were raised by their own family."

Her hand flew to her chest. "*You* are their family now."

He poured himself a drink and placed the stopper back on the decanter. "No, I'm just the unlucky bloke who was given guardianship over them."

Rearing back, she asked, "Is that how you truly feel? Unlucky?"

"Right now, that's exactly how I feel." He brought the glass up to his lips.

A long silence stretched out between them before she whispered, "You are not the man I thought you were."

He tightened his lips, but he made no attempt to respond to her.

Tears burned her eyes as she turned to leave. As she placed her hand on the door handle, she said, "I didn't think you would quit so easily."

She turned the handle and pushed the door open. She stepped out into the entry hall and attempted to compose herself. She couldn't very well show up to the nursery in tears or the girls would know that something was wrong.

Mr. Drake saw her from across the hall and rushed over to her. "He didn't fire you again, did he?"

"Not this time, no," she said with a shake of her head.

With kindness in his eyes, he asked, "Did he say something that upset you?"

"He did, but I believe it was because I expected too much of him."

Mr. Drake gave her an understanding nod as she brushed past him to walk up the stairs. If Lord Mountgarret didn't want Phoebe and Sophia, perhaps she could ask for guardianship over them. She could give them a lovely home; a home filled with love and laughter. They would be miserable in the Stewarts' home. Why couldn't Lord Mountgarret see that?

What a fool she had been! She had developed feelings for a man who cared little for others; a man who would give up guardianship so easily.

She'd been right. He was not the man she thought he was.

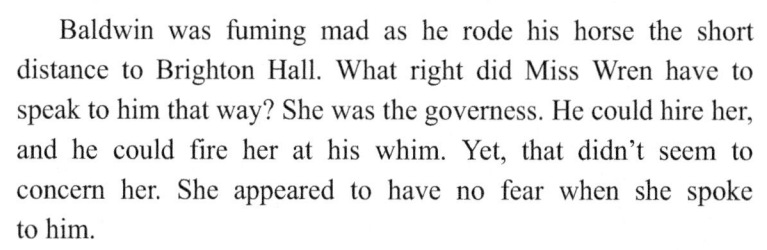

Baldwin was fuming mad as he rode his horse the short distance to Brighton Hall. What right did Miss Wren have to speak to him that way? She was the governess. He could hire her, and he could fire her at his whim. Yet, that didn't seem to concern her. She appeared to have no fear when she spoke to him.

What Miss Wren failed to realize was that he wasn't going to give up guardianship because he didn't care for the girls. No, he cared deeply for them, which meant he wanted to do what was best for them. If that meant they should be raised by their own family, then so be it.

Why did Miss Wren have to be so infuriating, he wondered, as he reined in his horse in front of the medieval castle. She was so insistent that his wards be given time to play and have fun. But that was wrong. Life had a way of beating you down, and it's only through hard work can you rise again. That's what he wanted his wards to learn.

A footman rushed down the steps to collect his horse. After he dismounted, he hurried up the steps towards the main door. It opened, and the butler tipped his head towards him.

"Welcome to Brighton Hall, Lord Mountgarret."

"May I ask where the duchess is?"

"She's in the study with the duke."

"Thank you."

He walked the short distance to the study in the rear of the castle and stepped inside the room. His eyes took in the room, and he saw Penelope sitting at her writing desk and Nicholas hunched over his desk.

He cleared his throat. "Did I come at a bad time?"

Penelope glanced up with a smile on her face. "Not at all. It is always a pleasure to see my favorite cousin."

Walking further into the study, he announced, "I have something important I need to speak to you about."

"Finally," Nicholas huffed. "I have been gravely concerned about your cravats. They can be quite the distraction."

He glanced down at his perfectly tied cravat. "What's wrong with my cravat?"

"I see that you are past hope, then," Nicholas said with a melodramatic sigh.

Ignoring his friend, he brought his gaze back to Penelope. "That's not why I am here."

Penelope smiled up at him. "Did you offer for Miss Wren then?"

Baldwin was stunned into silence for a moment. "What… heavens, no!" he shouted. "Why would you think that?"

"It's evident that you have feelings for her," she said.

He shook his head. "I do not have feelings for Miss Wren," he lied.

Nicholas leaned back in his chair. "Ah, you're in denial."

"I am not in denial. Miss Wren is just the governess."

Penelope pressed her lips together. "She is more than *just* a governess, cousin. She is my friend," she said in a chastising tone.

He sighed. "Regardless, that's not why I'm here."

"Perhaps you can tell us why you're here, so we don't have to keep guessing," Nicholas suggested.

Baldwin came around the sofa and sat down. "A relative of Phoebe and Sophia has come forth and requested guardianship over them."

Neither Penelope nor Nicholas spoke, so he added, "They're

staying at Rumney Manor as my guests until I decide what I should do with the girls."

"That's rubbish!" Nicholas shouted. "*You* are their rightful guardian!"

"I know, but…"

Nicholas shouted over him. "You can't just discard them so easily."

"I'm not!" Baldwin exclaimed.

"Well, it appears that way to me," Nicholas defended. "You never wanted them, and now you're willing to pawn them off onto someone else."

Baldwin jumped up from his chair. "That's not what is happening."

"Isn't it?" Nicholas growled.

"No!" he proclaimed. "I want to keep the girls! But I'm not sure if I am the best person to raise them."

Nicholas shook his head. "You're unbelievable."

Penelope rose from her seat and stepped closer to him. "Perhaps if you start from the beginning so we can better understand your reasoning."

"My reason is simple," Baldwin began, "I believe the girls might be better off being raised by their own family."

"And why do you say that?" Penelope asked gently.

He met her gaze. "Would you have been better off being raised by my mother than being the ward of the Duke of Blackbourne?"

"I see the issue," Penelope remarked as she sat down on the settee. "Yes, I would have been better off being raised by my aunt, but I believe fate intervened. After all, if I hadn't been the ward of the Duke of Blackbourne, then I doubt I would have ever met Nicholas."

His shoulders slumped slightly. "I'm a bachelor who keeps long hours in Town. How am I fit to raise two girls?"

"Find yourself a wife," Nicholas suggested.

He huffed. "That would just create a whole host of new problems."

"I disagree. Marrying Penelope was the best decision that I ever made," Nicholas said.

"Thank you, husband."

The duke smiled lovingly at his wife. "It's true. I have never been so blissfully happy."

"Can we get back to the matter at hand?" Baldwin drawled. "I need your advice."

Nicholas frowned. "My answer is simple. Keep the girls."

"But am I being selfish?"

Penelope considered him for a moment, then said carefully, "Their father granted you guardianship for a reason. Why do you suppose that was?"

"I am the girls' godfather."

She shook her head. "I doubt that's the only reason."

He stared at her with a bewildered look on his face. "I can't think of another one."

"Children become your greatest treasures," Penelope said, placing a hand over her stomach. "You would do anything for your children, including laying down your own life. So why would the girls' father list *you* as a guardian?"

"I suppose Thomas trusted me to do right by his girls. To educate them and introduce them into Society," he answered.

Penelope gave him a weak smile. "He also wanted you to love the girls, and to put their needs above your own, which, by the way, you are doing now by trying to figure out what is best for them."

Nicholas spoke up. "Besides, if Thomas wanted his relatives to be guardians to Phoebe and Sophia then he would have made his intentions known in his will."

"Mrs. Stewart's father had a falling out with the family. She and Thomas hardly spoke growing up."

"Have you considered allowing this Mrs. Stewart to be a part of their lives, but not their guardian?" Penelope asked.

"That might work," he mused.

Nicholas rose from his seat and came to sit next to Penelope. "I believe it would be a grave mistake to hand over guardianship to Mrs. Stewart. These girls have already become a part of *our* family now. They are a part of my crew."

"The girls actually described you as 'nice'," Baldwin said, chuckling.

"I *am* nice," Nicholas defended.

"That's not a word I would use to describe you," he joked.

"Well, there are many reasons I'm not nice to you."

Baldwin chuckled.

Placing his arm around Penelope's shoulder, Nicholas asked, "May I ask what you are going to do about Miss Wren leaving?"

"I offered her an increase in wages. What more could I do?"

"You could offer for her?" Nicholas suggested.

He shook his head. "Just think of the scandal that would arise if I married my wards' governess. Everyone would be convinced that I am exactly like my father."

"You are nothing like your father," Penelope contended. "He was cruel, spiteful, and didn't care about anyone else but himself."

"I know that, but my father's roguery was well known amongst the *ton*."

The duke grew serious. "The difference is that Penelope and I will endorse this marriage, and no one would *dare* challenge me."

"Regardless, Miss Wren hates me right now."

"Why?"

"We fought over Phoebe being able to play with frogs."

Penelope lifted her brow. "If I recall correctly, we used to play with frogs down by the pond growing up."

"But it's different," he contested.

"In what way?" Penelope asked.

"Phoebe shouldn't be frolicking around in the woodlands when she has lessons that she could be tending to."

Penelope frowned. "That's balderdash. Experiencing new things is important at Phoebe's age. Besides, I knew a girl that loved to climb trees growing up, and I daresay that playing with frogs is far safer than climbing trees."

"You're beginning to sound like Miss Wren," Baldwin muttered.

"Good, at least someone is," she replied unapologetically.

He rose. "If you will excuse me, I need some time to mull over my decision."

Nicholas rose as well. "Whatever you decide, we will support you. However, don't be a ninnyhammer."

"Thank you for your advice," he said as he departed.

Riding away from Brighton Hall, he knew what he was going to do about his wards, but he had no idea what he was going to do about Miss Wren.

14

BALDWIN DROPPED ONTO A SOFA IN HIS LIBRARY. HE'D JUST come from the most dreadfully boring dinner with the Stewarts and Mr. Baker. He was sure that it was boring because Miss Wren and the girls were noticeably absent. The only topics discussed were ones of polite conversation. To add to his misery, Mrs. Stewart had gone on at great length about how lovely the weather was in Cardiff.

Earlier, Miss Wren had sent word that she intended to eat dinner in the nursery with Sophia. After he'd received the note, he'd ordered that an additional tray was to be sent up for Phoebe. He didn't want her to go hungry.

A book of fables sat on the table in front of him, and he picked it up. Miss Wren must be reading this, he thought, as he rifled through the pages. No wonder she believed in such silly nonsense. He hoped she wasn't reading these stories to the girls.

The door to the library opened, and he glanced over to see Sophia slowly closing the door. She turned, saw him, and her face paled slightly.

Lifting his brow, he asked, "May I ask what you're doing, young lady?"

"I came down for a book," she admitted slowly.

"Where is Miss Wren?"

"She fell asleep while she was reading us a book of French poems."

Baldwin grinned. "I can see why. French poems can be rather boring."

She giggled.

Gesturing towards the shelves of books, he asked, "Can I help you find one?"

She stepped closer to him. "I want to find the book that Miss Wren was reading to us yesterday. It's called *Aesop's Fables*."

He held up the book. "This book?"

"Yes, my lord."

Hearing 'my lord' out of the little girl's mouth sounded wrong. "I don't want to hear you ever call me 'my lord' or Lord Mountgarret again," he said gently.

"What may I call you then?"

He paused. "I suppose you may call me Baldwin."

She shook her head. "Miss Wren would never allow that."

"Then it shall be our little secret."

A smile came to her lips.

He waved her closer. "Would you like me to read to you?"

"I would, very much," she responded eagerly as she came around the sofa and sat down next to him.

He opened the book to a story entitled *The Boy Who Cried Wolf*. He showed Sophia the picture, and she leaned closer.

"Have you read this one?" he asked.

She shook her head. "Not yet."

"Good."

As he started reading the story, he noticed that Sophia moved closer and closer to him until no space was between them. He placed his arm around her shoulder, and she rested her head on his chest.

Once the story was done, he moved on to the next story and

then the next. It wasn't until he noticed her deep breathing that he put the book down. At some point, Sophia had fallen asleep on him.

The door to the library opened, and Miss Wren entered swiftly. Her eyes scanned the room, and he saw a brief look of panic come over her.

"Are you looking for something, Miss Wren?" he asked softly so as not to disturb Sophia.

In a worried tone, she admitted, "I can't find Sophia."

With his free hand, he indicated the girl was sleeping on his chest. Miss Wren let out a sigh of relief. "I've been looking everywhere for her," she said as she came around the sofa and extended her hands. "I'll take her back to the nursery, my lord."

"That's not necessary," he said, rising carefully with Sophia cradled gently in his arms. "I'll take her."

"You?" Miss Wren repeated.

"Yes, me."

She stepped back. "Of course. Thank you."

They walked up the stairs in silence, and Miss Wren stepped in front of him to open the door to the nursery. He went and laid Sophia on the bed, covering her with the quilt. He then glanced over and saw Phoebe sleeping peacefully in her bed. He took a moment to place a kiss on their small foreheads before he departed.

Miss Wren followed him into the hall and closed the door. "Thank you for carrying Sophia up to her bed."

Turning to face her, he replied, "You're welcome."

Miss Wren began wringing her hands. "I would like to apologize for Sophia sneaking off to the library. I had been reading the girls poems in French, and I must have dozed off."

"I'm not upset with you," he replied in a reassuring tone.

She visibly relaxed enough to smile, which he returned. "I'm glad."

"As I stated before, I am not a monster."

"No, you are definitely not."

They stood there, looking at each other, saying nothing, until he cleared his throat. "Good night, Miss Wren."

"Good night, Lord Mountgarret."

He took a couple of steps down the hall, but something compelled him to turn back around.

"Is everything all right?" Miss Wren asked.

He took a step closer to her. "Are you still angry with me?"

"I find that my ire dissipates rather quickly when I'm around you," she admitted, looking away.

"That pleases me."

She met his gaze, and he admired her steadfast green eyes. "It does?"

He nodded. "I'm no longer angry with you, either."

"You were angry with me?"

Baldwin felt like kicking himself for saying something so stupid. "It was only a trifling thing."

She grinned. "I suppose I anger you quite frequently."

"That you do." He hoped his grin would take any possible sting out of his words.

He took a step closer. "How can I convince you to stay on as our governess?" She shook her head, so he rushed to add, "I shall give you anything you ask."

She hesitated. "Anything?"

"Anything at all," he rushed out.

Squaring her shoulders, she replied, "If you retain guardianship of the girls, I will stay until the end of the year."

Baldwin felt as if a huge weight had been lifted off his shoulders. He closed the distance between them and pulled her into his arms. "Thank you, Miss Wren. You have made me immensely happy."

At first, she stood rigid in his arms, but after only a moment, he felt her soften, felt her exhale deeply, and sink against him. *This is a promising sign*, he thought to himself.

"Does that mean you've decided to keep the girls?"

He kissed the top of her head before he lowered his arms. "I shall need to speak to the Stewarts first before I make my final decision."

Miss Wren tilted her lovely face to look up at him, and he realized that he was in more trouble than he thought. He wasn't just beguiled by the lovely governess. No, at some point, he had fallen hopelessly in love with her.

He took a staggering step back at that realization and hastily said, "Evening, Miss Wren."

Without waiting for her response, he swiftly headed down the hall towards his bedchamber. Perhaps Nicholas had been right. Maybe he should just offer for her and be done with this misery?

He stepped into his bedchamber and closed the door. A smile came to his lips as he realized he had convinced Miss Wren to stay until the end of the year, assuming everything went according to his plan tomorrow with the Stewarts. That should give him plenty of time to woo her slowly. With the Duke and Duchess of Blackbourne's endorsement, no one would dare criticize Miss Wren or his decision to marry her.

Baldwin reined in his horse near the front of Rumney Manor and dismounted. He handed off the reins to a waiting footman and headed up the stairs towards the main door.

Drake greeted him from the entryway. "Did you have a good morning ride, milord?"

"I did," he said, removing his gloves and extending them towards the butler. "Will you inform Mr. and Mrs. Stewart and Mr. Baker that I wish to speak with them in the study?"

The butler tipped his head. "As you wish."

He started walking across the entry hall but stopped and spun back around. "And ensure that Miss Wren is invited, as well."

"It shall be done, milord."

"Thank you," he said, resuming his walk.

Once in his study, Baldwin stepped around his desk and sat down. He started looking through a stack of papers that needed his signatures. He might as well get some work done while he waited for them to all assemble, he thought.

After signing his name to nearly ten documents, Mr. and Mrs. Stewart and Mr. Baker walked into the room.

He rose from his chair and buttoned his riding jacket. "Thank you for coming so quickly."

Mrs. Stewart smiled. "It's our pleasure, my lord."

"We're just waiting on Miss Wren, then we will proceed with the meeting," he informed them.

"Miss Wren? The governess?" Mrs. Stewart questioned in a haughty tone.

He nodded. "Yes, I value Miss Wren's opinion quite highly, if you must know."

Pointing towards a chair, he encouraged, "Please take a seat, Mrs. Stewart."

"Thank you," she said, moving gracefully to sit on an upholstered armchair. Her husband moved to stand behind her and placed his hand on her shoulder.

Dressed in a white gown with a yellow sash tied around her waist, Miss Wren walked hesitantly into the room. "Mr. Drake informed me that you wish to speak to me, my lord."

He smiled encouragingly. "That's true. Please take a seat, Miss Wren."

Once Miss Wren was situated, Baldwin walked in front of the group and announced, "I have made my decision regarding guardianship over the girls."

Mr. Baker stepped closer to the Stewarts in anticipation of his remarks.

"I've decided that Phoebe and Sophia will remain in my care and under my protection," he stated, pausing to let his words sink in.

Mrs. Stewart's face paled. "You would deprive the girls of their family, their own flesh and blood?"

"No, I would not," he replied. "I strongly encourage you to continue building your relationship with the girls. You both will always be welcome at Rumney Manor. Perhaps in the future, when they are more comfortable, Phoebe and Sophia could come spend time in Worchester."

"But you are unwed!" Mr. Stewart contended. "We can provide a home that is stable and nurturing for the girls, whereas you only have servants to raise them."

He put his hand up. "I'm still not entirely sure why Thomas granted me guardianship over his girls, but I intend to honor my late friend's wish by taking care of his greatest treasures."

Mrs. Stewart glanced disapprovingly over at Miss Wren and said, "You would rather have an unfit governess teach the girls than their own relation?"

Baldwin frowned. "In no way is Miss Wren unfit to teach Phoebe and Sophia. Furthermore, I will play a more active role in rearing these girls so they each can become accomplished ladies," he argued.

"Do you take umbrage with us owning a pig farm?" Mr. Stewart asked.

"Not at all," Baldwin replied.

Mrs. Stewart rose from her chair, and with tears in her eyes, she pleaded, "Please, let us raise Phoebe and Sophia. We have no children of our own, and we would be good to them."

Baldwin shook his head. "I'm sorry, but I've made my decision."

A hard expression came to Mr. Stewart's face. "We should have anticipated you had no honor, especially since it is abundantly clear you are having a dalliance with the governess."

"I beg your pardon!" Miss Wren exclaimed as she jumped up from her seat.

Mr. Stewart turned his fiery gaze towards her. "This is your fault. If the girls left, then you would be out of a job. You seduced him with your feminine charms."

Miss Wren's mouth gaped. "I did no such thing!"

"You are out of line, Mr. Stewart!" Baldwin growled.

Straightening to his full height, Mr. Stewart declared, "I am not. We shall petition Parliament for custody of Phoebe and Sophia, and we will cite your disreputable behavior."

"That is your right, but you might want to consider that the Duke of Blackbourne supports my decision to retain guardianship."

Mr. Stewart's eyes flickered with uncertainty for only a moment before he stated, "I see you surround yourself with unscrupulous people. After all, everyone knows that the Duke of Blackbourne killed his own brother to become the heir."

Baldwin took a commanding step closer to Mr. Stewart, and he was gratified to see fear in the man's eyes. "How dare you make false accusations about my dear friend in my own home!"

Mr. Baker spoke up from next to Mrs. Stewart. "Perhaps our emotions have gotten the best of us. Why don't we sit down and talk about this like rational adults?"

"That's a good idea, Mr. Baker," Baldwin said, glaring at Mr. Stewart.

In a huff, Mr. Stewart stepped towards the window and stared out.

Mrs. Stewart offered him a force smile. "We are clearly upset because we had hoped we would have been given guardianship of Phoebe and Sophia."

"I do respect your emotions, Mrs. Stewart. However, I cannot accept your horrendous insults towards Miss Wren and the Duke of Blackbourne," he replied.

"What if we took the girls on a trial basis?" Mrs. Stewart suggested.

"No."

She tried again. "We could take them for a month and see how they adjust to their surroundings."

He shook his head. "My answer is still no."

"But the girls love me," Mrs. Stewart attempted in a shrill voice.

Baldwin saw Miss Wren attempting to stifle a smile at Mrs. Stewart's last comment. She was failing miserably.

"Be that as it may, the girls will remain with me," he stated.

A knock came at the door.

"Enter," Baldwin called.

His man of business, Henry, strode into the room with wrinkled clothing and disheveled hair.

"Are you feeling well?" Baldwin asked, concerned.

Henry nodded. "I am. I apologize for my appearance, but I've been riding since dawn."

"From where?"

"Worchester," Henry replied, his eyes drifting towards Mrs. Stewart. "I discovered the most interesting information about the Stewarts."

Baldwin lifted his brow. "Which is?"

"The Stewarts do own a rather large pig farm, but the majority of the pigs have died from some type of disease," Henry shared.

Mr. Stewart bobbed his head. "It's true. Sadly, most of the pigs have contracted a disease that's been killing them off, one by one."

"I am sorry to hear that," Baldwin replied sincerely.

"Thank you," Mr. Stewart said. "It has been a trying time."

Henry came to stand next to him. "Furthermore, I learned that the Stewarts have fired most of their household staff."

Mrs. Stewart nodded. "That's also true. During this difficult time, we were unable to afford to keep our large household staff."

"Gaining guardianship over Miss Phoebe and Miss Sophia would have solved all their financial problems," Henry stated. "They would have been given a monthly allowance to support the girls and their own lifestyle."

"How dare you stand there and imply the only reason why we would want the girls was because of their monthly allowance!" Mrs. Stewart exclaimed.

Henry turned to face Baldwin. "I would also like to note that Mrs. Stewart is a liar."

"How dare you!" Mr. Stewart exclaimed. "My wife is no such thing."

Huffing, Henry said, "Mrs. Stewart is not related to Thomas Barrington as she claims, but she is the daughter of a local gentleman in Worcester. A man known as Robert Baker."

"Baker?" he questioned, his eyes seeking out Mr. Baker.

Henry nodded. "Yes, Walter Baker is his son, as well."

"That's preposterous!" Mrs. Stewart declared, her eyes growing frantic.

Henry reached into his jacket pocket and pulled out a handful of crumpled papers. "I have signed affidavits from people in the village confirming my claims."

"Clearly, this man is lying!" Mr. Stewart shouted.

"My friend is many things, Mr. Stewart, but a liar is not one of them," Baldwin stated in a steely tone. "How dare you come into my home and lie to me! You have five minutes to leave my estate before I send for the constable and have you arrested."

With gratification, he watched the Stewarts as they hurried out of the room with Mr. Baker on their heels. However, he wasn't finished with the solicitor just yet.

"Mr. Baker!"

Mr. Baker stopped his retreat and spun around, fear in his eyes.

He took a commanding step towards him. "Did you coax them, or did they make up their own elaborate story?" he demanded.

Refusing to make eye-contact, Mr. Baker muttered, "I may have coaxed them a little."

"A little!" he exclaimed. "I suggest you start looking for a new line of work, because I intend to do everything in my power to ensure that you are discredited as a solicitor."

Without saying another word, Mr. Baker ran out of the room.

Baldwin stared at his man of business in amazement as he ran a hand through his hair. "How did you discover the truth?"

Henry smiled smugly. "I went into Worchester and stopped for a drink at the public house. There was a man at my table who was already into his cups. He turned out to be the former under-butler at the Stewart's estate. After buying him a few drinks, he was more than willing to spill all the information on his employers."

"Who else did you speak to?" Baldwin asked, glancing down at the crumpled pieces of paper still in Henry's hand.

Henry chuckled as he dropped the papers onto the table. "I lied. I just grabbed a few pieces of paper from the public house and shoved them into my pocket."

"That was genius!" Miss Wren praised.

Henry gave her a suave smile and bowed. "You must be Miss Wren, the governess that I've heard so much about."

She curtsied. "I am, but I'm worried about what Lord Mountgarret has said about me. He has already informed me that I am both vexing and infuriating."

"I assure you that he has spoken only good things, Miss Wren." Henry chuckled. "Allow me to introduce myself. My name is Henry Barnet, and I am Lord Mountgarret's man of business."

With a heavy sigh, Baldwin said, "I can't believe I almost gave up custody to those two unscrupulous crooks. I was so easily fooled by their sad story." He turned towards his friend. "How can I possibly thank you for what you've done?"

"You owe me nothing," Henry assured him with a smile.

Baldwin shook his head. "I will find a way to repay you."

"No payment is necessary, but I would like to meet your wards," Henry suggested.

"Oh, I can help with that." Miss Wren stepped over to the servant's passageway. She slid open the panel and ordered, "Come on out, girls. There's someone we want you to meet."

Phoebe and Sophia stepped out of the passageway with wide smiles on their faces. They didn't even appear abashed for being caught eavesdropping. They immediately ran over to Baldwin and threw their arms around him.

"Thank you for keeping us," Phoebe said.

Baldwin wrapped his arms around them. "We're a family now, and nothing is ever going to change that." He smiled at Miss Wren and mouthed, "Thank you."

She returned his smile, and he saw tears forming in her eyes. How he loved this woman!

He dropped his arms to his side and provided the introductions. "Girls, I would like to introduce you to Henry Barnet. He was the one who saved you from the Stewarts and their web of lies."

Both girls curtsied and murmured, "Thank you, Mr. Barnet."

As the girls started asking Henry all types of questions, Baldwin stepped closer to Miss Wren and asked, "Would you care to take a stroll around the gardens after the girls' midday meal?"

"I think I can arrange that."

"That pleases me."

His first step was completed. He had retained guardianship of the girls. Now, the next step might take a little more work. He somehow needed to convince Miss Wren to become his wife.

15

"Why can't we take a walk in the garden with you?" Phoebe asked, pouting just a little.

"Because Lord Mountgarret asked me to join him on a stroll after your midday meal," Emeline replied, placing the final pin in her hair.

"Are you sure that we weren't invited?" Sophia spoke up from next to her, sounding doubtful.

Crouching down, Emeline kissed Sophia's forehead. "I'm sure, my darling."

"Do you think he's going to fire you again?" Phoebe questioned.

"I don't think so," Emeline shared with a smile. "With all this excitement, I forgot to tell you that I have agreed to stay on as your governess until the end of the year."

Both girls cheered.

"Settle down, girls," she chastised lightly. "Betty is going to be here any minute to stay with you while you work on your geography lessons."

"I hate geography," Phoebe complained.

She laughed. "Seems to me that you hate all your lessons."

"That's not true," Phoebe contended. "I enjoy our botany lessons, when we walk through the woodlands."

Sophia smiled. "I like those, too."

"Hm. That's good to know," Emeline said, nodding sagely. "Next time we walk through the woodlands, I believe all the instruction will be given in French. That way we can practice both at the same time."

Phoebe groaned. "I hate French."

"Why did I have the feeling you were going to say that?" Emeline grinned.

The door opened, and the young maid walked into the room with a smile on her face. "Mrs. Garvey asked me to come stay with the girls while you go on a romantic walk with Lord Mountgarret."

The girls giggled, covering their mouths with their hands.

"It's not a romantic walk," Emeline contended. "We're just two adults taking a stroll in the gardens." She picked up her straw bonnet off the table and loosely tied the strings. "I shall be back shortly."

As she walked down the hall, she wondered why Lord Mountgarret wanted to speak to her. She knew he wasn't going to fire her. Perhaps he just wanted to speak about the girls' lessons. Yes, that must be it. Why else would he want a moment alone with her?

She wouldn't mind if he kissed her again, but she doubted that was the purpose of this visit. It was abundantly clear that Lord Mountgarret regretted kissing her in the first place. However, no matter what he thought, she would never regret her actions. She'd found his kiss to be perfect. Absolutely perfect.

At the bottom of the stairs in the entry hall, Lord Mountgarret was waiting for her. He was dressed in a green jacket, white waistcoat, and tan trousers. He offered her a dashing smile as she descended the stairs. She watched as he perused the length of her body, and in his eyes, she saw approval, making her feel desirable.

She came to a stop in front of him, and he gazed at her face as he murmured, "You're looking especially lovely today, Miss Wren."

A blush came to her cheeks. "Thank you, Lord Mountgarret."

He offered his arm and escorted her towards the rear of the estate. "I'm glad to see that you wore a bonnet. It is rather warm outside today."

She glanced over at him with a playful grin. "Dear heavens, are we only going to speak about polite conversation on this stroll?"

He chuckled. "No, it was merely an observation."

A footman standing near the rear door opened it for them. As they stepped into the well-maintained gardens, she scanned the shrubbery and colorful plants divided by the footpaths.

"I would say that the gardens are beautiful, but I feel as though you would believe my comments to be ingenuine," she joked.

He smiled at her. "It's amazing to me that just a few months ago, the garden was in horrible shape. The gardeners have been working hard to restore them to their former glory."

"They certainly have," she agreed.

"I would like to apologize to you," Baldwin said as he led her down a footpath.

"For what in particular?"

He brought his free hand up and placed it over hers. "After I heard the Stewarts' sad story, it reminded me so much of my own past, and I sympathized with them. I'm afraid it clouded my judgement."

"You were manipulated by them. They knew about your past and exploited it."

"That's true, but I should have known better." He stopped on the path and turned to face her. "You tried to warn me about Mrs.

Stewart, but I didn't believe you. And for that, I am truly, deeply sorry."

Emeline could hear the remorse in his voice. "It is all right," she assured him. "I understand why you did it. You had a tough decision to make."

"I did, but I promise I will never discount what you say again."

"Thank you. That means a lot."

A smirk came to his lips. "I can't believe you forgave me so easily. I had worked out a whole speech of how wrong I was, and I intended to grovel."

"Grovel?" she repeated, smiling. "I would have liked to see that."

"I guess you will never see it now." Lord Mountgarret resumed walking. "When I first arrived at Rumney Manor, I came with the intention of ensuring the girls were being well taken care of, and then I fully intended to leave them in the hands of their governess. But that has all changed because of you." He glanced at her. "You were insistent that I spent time with them and get to know them."

She nodded. "Phoebe and Sophia just want to be loved."

"I think that's a wish that everyone secretly has."

"I agree."

He stepped off the path and led her towards a cluster of trees in the corner of the gardens. "I'm relieved that you agreed to stay until the end of the year."

"It's the least I can do," she stated. "I've grown to care for those girls immensely."

"I know you have, and the girls are lucky to have you in their lives."

With a side-glance at him, she replied, "I would say the same thing about you."

Lord Mountgarret stopped at the edge of the trees and dropped his arm. He looked at her, and lines darkened his handsome features. "There's something else that I wish to discuss with you."

She gave him a small, reassuring smile, but he still did not speak. They stared at each other for an endless moment, yet his enigmatic expression gave away nothing of his thoughts.

"Are you feeling all right?" she asked finally.

"I am," he said. "For the first time, I have clarity in my life. I finally know where I belong."

"That's wonderful," she gushed.

He took a step closer, and she had to tilt her head to look up at him. "It is."

"And where is it that you belong?"

Something flickered in the depth of his eyes. "With you."

She took a deep breath, fearing that she had misheard him. "What are you saying?"

He closed the distance between them and cupped her right cheek. "I have never met a more infuriating young woman than you..." he paused, "but I have never met a more kind-hearted, compassionate person either. You challenge me in ways I never thought possible."

The tip of his thumb caressed her cheekbone.

"The girls need a mother," he said softly.

She blinked in surprise. "The girls?"

"Yes, and I believe you're the perfect candidate for the position."

Emeline furrowed her brows together as she attempted to formulate her thoughts. "If I understand this correctly, you want to marry me so I can be the girls' mother."

"Yes, but also because we get along nicely. Don't we?" he asked with a boyish grin.

She opened her mouth and closed it. "You are asking me to commit to a marriage of convenience, then?"

"What?" he asked. "No, that is not what I meant."

She stepped back, and his hand dropped from her cheek.

"That's what it sounded like to me, Lord Mountgarret," she said, trying to keep the hurt out of her voice.

"I'd prefer that you call me Baldwin," he said, running a hand through his hair.

"That is inappropriate, Lord Mountgarret," she replied with a shake of her head.

He gave her a look of disbelief. "I believe we are past formalities, Emeline. After all, I am attempting to offer for you."

Nervousness caused Emeline to start wringing her hands together. "We hardly know each other," she responded.

"That's true, but I know everything I need to know about you."

She shook her head vehemently. "That is not true. There is still so much that I haven't told you about me."

"It wouldn't change the way how I feel about you."

"I believe it would."

He reached for her hands. "I love you, Emeline." She stood rooted to her spot as he stared deep into her eyes. "Did you hear me? I love you."

Pressing her lips together, she blinked back the tears filling her eyes. "There are things about my past that could change everything between us."

"Then tell me," he said. "Tell me everything that I need to know about Emeline Wren."

A tear slid down her cheek as she gathered the strength to tell him the truth. Would he hate her when she finally revealed it?

"The truth is…"

A man's voice broke through their private interlude. "Pardon me, milord. But a man named Mr. Warren is looking for his daughter, and he has asked to speak to you."

Without removing his gaze from her, Baldwin stated firmly, "I'm afraid I don't know a Mr. Warren. Send him away."

Slipping her hands out of his, Emeline turned her attention to the liveried footman. "Please tell Mr. Warren I will speak to him in the drawing room."

The footman tipped his head. "As you wish, Miss Wren."

She shifted her gaze back towards Baldwin. He was looking at her with a puzzled expression. "Why would you speak to this man?"

"Because," she hesitated, "he *is* my father."

Baldwin reared back. "Your father?"

Emeline squared her shoulders and admitted, "My name is Emeline Warren, and I am the daughter of Mr. Hugh Warren, the owner of Warren Trading Company."

"Would you mind repeating that?" Baldwin growled.

Emeline gave him a tentative smile. "My name is Emeline Warren, and the man who has come to call is my father."

Turning his back to her, she heard him mutter curse words under his breath. She waited for him to say something, anything, to her, but he refused to turn back to face her.

"I know you are angry with me…"

"What a perceptive young woman you are," he replied dryly as he turned to face her.

Ignoring his critical tone, she tried again. "I had no choice but to run away from my home. My stepmother had planned to imprison me in my bedchamber if I didn't marry a suitor of her choice. If that hadn't worked, she planned to have me committed to Bedlam."

"You're a good liar," he responded with a shake of his head. "Quite believable, in fact."

"I'm not lying. It was the only way to stay safe," she contended.

Baldwin took a step back, creating further distance between

them. "Only a male relation can send someone to Bedlam. Everyone knows that."

"I was not aware of that," she replied, frowning. "Regardless, I overheard my stepmother saying she'd found two doctors who would confirm my 'hysteria'."

He shifted his gaze away from her. "So, it makes it all right to deceive me?"

"I never said that. I know it was wrong of me to deceive you." She glanced over at Rumney Manor. "I will explain everything after I have spoken to my father."

He flicked his wrist towards the estate. "Go. I'll be here when you are finished."

"I never meant to hurt you, Baldwin," she said, biting her lower lip.

He stiffened. "I would prefer it if we had formality between us, Miss Warren."

"As you wish, my lord," she murmured, her voice hitching.

She reluctantly turned towards Rumney Manor and hurried down the footpath to the rear of the estate. The door was opened for her by the footman, and she stepped inside. She felt the tears burning in her eyes, and she wiped them away with the sleeve of her gown. She knew she needed to compose herself before facing her father, so she found a corner to hide in.

Mrs. Garvey was about to walk past her when she stopped and asked, "Are you all right, dear?"

She shook her head and tears escaped from her eyes. "My father just showed up, and Lord Mountgarret is furious that I deceived him."

"Would you like me to speak to Lord Mountgarret? After all, I was the one who suggested we change your name."

"That's not necessary, but I thank you for the offer."

Mrs. Garvey pulled her into a loving embrace. "These things have a way of working themselves out."

"I don't think this one can be fixed," Emeline said forlornly.

"Time will tell." Mrs. Garvey leaned back and looked her in the eye. "Don't give up on Lord Mountgarret. He cares for you deeply."

"He hates me," she admitted.

"No, he most assuredly does not." The kind housekeeper stepped back. "It's time to go face your father."

She nodded. "He will be angry with me, as well."

"I have no doubt that he will be furious, but it's a parent's job to worry about their child. Now, go," Mrs. Garvey ordered, "and I will send up refreshments to the drawing room."

Emeline walked across the entry hall but stopped outside of the drawing room, taking a shuddering breath. She could do this.

She stepped into the drawing room and saw her father staring out the window. He hadn't heard her come in, and she took just a moment to look at him. He hadn't changed much since she last saw him, except for the hair around his temples had turned grey.

"Father..." she started, her voice barely above a whisper.

He turned to face her, and the relief was evident on his sharp features.

"Emeline," he said, almost reverently. "Thank goodness." He closed the distance between them in a few strides and wrapped her up in his arms. "I was so scared. I thought I'd lost you."

Tucking her face into his shoulder, she replied, "You will never lose me, Father."

He leaned back but kept her in his arms. "What were you thinking, my impulsive child? Don't you realize what could have happened to you?"

"I do, but I was perfectly safe here at Rumney Manor."

"Thank heavens for that."

"When did you arrive home?"

"Earlier today. The moment my coach came to a stop, Harry informed me that you had run away to his sister's estate because my wife threatened to send you to Bedlam." He dropped his arms. "Did I miss anything?"

"Did you speak to Priscilla?"

He nodded. "I did. However, she was in hysterics about you running away. She said she'd been frantically searching for you, discreetly, of course."

"I doubt that."

He gave her a disapproving look. "Why do you say that?"

Emeline stepped over to a velvet settee and sat down. "Before I left, I overheard Priscilla and Juliet talking about me."

"You were eavesdropping."

"I was," she admitted. "Priscilla wanted me to marry Lord Mortain."

"Mortain? But he is my age."

"That's what I said, but that didn't matter to Priscilla. She intended to lock me in my bedchamber until I agreed to marry him."

He came to sit down next to her. "Little did Priscilla realize how stubborn you are. Besides, I know all this. Harry already informed me of Priscilla's intentions." He frowned. "Still, you shouldn't just run away, Emeline," he said, his voice rising. "That's no way to handle challenges in your life."

She shifted in her seat to face him. "Why? That's what you do," she challenged.

"I beg your pardon?"

"You always leave! You're never home. Each time you leave, I've had to contend with Priscilla, who hates me."

"She doesn't hate you…"

Emeline spoke over him. "She does! Priscilla criticizes everything that I do, everything I say, and everything that I wear. She's even commented about how loudly I walk in slippers."

"I understand it's hard for you…"

"No! You don't understand." Emeline jumped up from her seat. "You left me! Just like mother left me." She walked over to the window and looked out at the gardens. She saw Lord Mountgarret still standing next to the cluster of trees, waiting for her. A feeling of guilt crept into her heart. Would he ever forgive her for deceiving him?

Her father's voice came from behind her. "I'm sorry that you felt this way, Emie. I never meant to hurt you."

"Don't you love me anymore?" she asked, turning around to face him.

His lips were pressed tightly together. "How can you ask that question?"

"I need you in my life, Father," she murmured. "I can't lose you, too."

Tears came to her father's eyes. "Ever since your mother died, I've been trying to find a new purpose in my life. I miss your mother every day, and every time I look at your face, you remind me of her. I've buried myself in work because I miss your mother so desperately."

"I miss her, too."

He nodded. "I know you do. I married Priscilla to fill a void in your life, but I had no idea that it was so bad for you."

"It has been truly awful."

"Then, it's time I stop traveling."

"Truly?"

He placed his hands on her shoulders. "You are more important to me than anything, including my company. We'll return to Cairnwood Hall, and I'll make some changes."

"Do you mean it, Father?"

He smiled tenderly at her. "I do. I can't even imagine what you were thinking, fleeing to an estate in Cardiff. Please tell me that Mrs. Garvey has been good to you."

"Actually, Mrs. Garvey hired me as the governess to two wonderful girls."

He stared at her. "You were a governess?"

"I was," she admitted proudly.

He didn't look pleased. "That is unacceptable."

"It was only until my twenty-first birthday," she rushed to

add. "Then I could access my inheritance from Grandmother and find a place for myself."

Her father shook his head. "I'm surprised that Lord Mountgarret even allowed you to work in his home, considering you are my daughter."

Wincing, she admitted, "He didn't know who I was."

"How was that possible?"

"Mrs. Garvey suggested I go by the name of Miss Wren."

"You went by an assumed name?"

She nodded. "I did."

"I've known Lord Mountgarret to be an honorable man," her father said. "Did he treat you fairly?"

"He did."

"Good. Then I don't have to challenge him to a duel."

She smiled. "I assure you that his actions were entirely honorable."

"Why don't you go pack your trunks," he said with a smile, "and we shall depart for Cairnwood Hall?"

"I only brought a valise with me."

"Only a valise?" he repeated. "Well, I suppose that shall be easy enough to pack."

"May we depart tomorrow, instead?"

He nodded. "If that is what you wish, but I insist that we stay in the coaching inn in town. That way, we can begin our journey at dawn."

"I am amenable to that," she answered. "But first, I need to say goodbye to the girls and Lord Mountgarret."

"I thought Lord Mountgarret didn't know your true identity?"

She shifted her gaze towards the window. "He didn't until a few moments ago. But we became friends, so I feel I owe him an explanation."

"That's odd," her father muttered. "Generally, the master of the house does not become friends with the help."

"I know," she said, returning her gaze to his, "but Lord Mountgarret isn't like any gentleman of the *ton* that I have known. He is kind and thoughtful."

Her father eyed her suspiciously. "Are you sure that nothing has transpired between you two?"

"Nothing that you would deem inappropriate."

"That was not my question."

"I assure you that Lord Mountgarret will be relieved when I am gone," she replied, clasping her hands in front of her.

A maid stepped into the room with a tray in her hands. She placed it in the center of the table. After she poured two cups of tea, she stepped back and asked, "Is there anything else I can do for you, miss?"

"No, thank you," Emeline replied.

The maid curtsied and left the room.

Emeline started walking towards the door. "Allow me to say my goodbyes, and I will be down shortly."

"Does Lord Mountgarret have a library?"

"He does. Would you like me to show you?"

Her father reached down for a teacup. "Yes, please." He drank his tea in one long sip, then answered, "One can always occupy oneself with a good book." He put the empty cup down on the tray.

"Follow me," she said as she walked out into the entry hall.

As she walked down the familiar halls of Rumney Manor, she realized that it felt like home. But that didn't matter. This wasn't her home, no matter how much her heart ached for it to be.

16

BALDWIN HAD BEEN TRICKED BY EMELINE. HE WAS A FOOL. A blasted fool! He'd confided in her, trusted her, but she'd deceived him. Not only had she lied about her surname, but she was the daughter of his main competitor. How could she have done this to him?

He saw Emeline exit the rear of his estate and watched as she slowly passed through the gardens. If he was a smart man, he would just tell her to leave him in peace. But something held him back.

"I've come to apologize... again," she said, stopping a short distance away.

"Don't bother," he huffed. "It won't change anything."

"I know that I hurt you..." she replied, taking a step closer.

"Hurt me?" he repeated dryly. "Don't flatter yourself, Miss Wren."

He was surprised that his curt tone didn't seem to scare her.

"The lead groomsman at my estate is the brother of Mrs. Garvey," she explained calmly. "He indicated that I would be safe at Rumney Manor, which I was. Once I arrived, your housekeeper suggested I change my name to Wren in case my stepmother came looking for me. She was the one who hired me as the governess." Emeline clasped her hands in front of her. "I was only supposed to be the governess until another was hired."

"So, it was my housekeeper's fault that you deceived me?" She shook her head sadly. "No, it was entirely my fault."

Pursing his lips, Baldwin asked, "What is it that you want from me?"

"I want you to know that everything else I told you was the truth."

"You must excuse me if I don't believe you," he replied coldly.

Emeline looked at the ground. "I never intended for you to find out this way."

He took a step closer towards her, causing her to bring her gaze back up. "How exactly was I supposed to find out?"

"I started to tell you earlier, before we were interrupted."

"How convenient," he scoffed.

She looked up, earnestness burning brightly in her eyes. "I understand you're angry, but you have no right to treat me this way."

"I beg your pardon?"

She straightened her shoulders as she looked deeply into his eyes. "I made a mistake, but I am attempting to apologize."

"Is that supposed to make it right between us?"

"No, but it can be a start."

He pressed his lips together. "You have lost my trust, Miss Warren."

"I understand. Then I shall go."

"I believe that would be for the best."

Emeline turned to leave but stopped. Tentatively, she turned to face him. "Earlier today, you said…"

He spoke over her. "I know what I said."

"Did you mean it?"

He paused as he debated how to answer. He could lie to her

and tell her that she meant nothing to him. Or he could tell her that he still loved her, and a part of him always would.

"I believe I spoke out of turn," he finally said. "However, I am honor bound, should you desire to accept my offer of marriage."

The hurt on her features was evident as she stared down at her hands. "I would never trap you into a marriage of convenience."

"How kind of you," he drawled.

Her full lower lip trembled as she opened her mouth to speak. "Regardless of what you think of me, just know that you will always retain a place in my heart."

He was rendered speechless. He'd been cruel to her, and yet, she still spoke of loving him. How was that possible?

"I believe my job here is done," she murmured as tears began to roll down her cheeks. "I wanted to help you gain a relationship with Phoebe and Sophia, so you would love them dearly. I believe you love them almost as much as I do. I'm glad for that."

Some of his anger dissipated at the sight of her tears. "I cannot thank you enough for what you did for the girls… and me." He reached into his waistcoat pocket and fingered a few coins. "Shall I pay you the wages that you're due?"

She gave him a weak smile. "That's not necessary. On my twenty-first birthday, I shall inherit my grandmother's estate. I am an heiress, in my own right."

"That's why you were going to stay on as the governess only until your twenty-first birthday?" he asked.

"Yes. I never intended to stay at Rumney Manor for long. The truth is that I had originally planned to stay in Mrs. Garvey's cottage for the two months that I was here," she admitted. "Perhaps even *borrow* books from your library during my stay."

He took another step closer to her. "Why didn't you tell me the truth?"

"There was never an opportune time," she said, her eyes

imploring him to understand. "If you recall, after our first meeting, you fired me. Besides, if you had discovered who I truly was, would you have allowed me to work for you as a governess?"

He shook his head. "No, I wouldn't have."

"That's what I assumed."

His eyes shifted towards the second level of Rumney Manor. "Have you told the girls yet?"

Briefly, she lowered her gaze. "No, I haven't. I was hoping we could tell them together."

"They'll be devastated to learn that you're leaving."

Emeline spoke so softly that he barely made out her words. "No more than I will be at leaving them."

"When do you plan to depart?"

She swiped at the tears rolling down her cheeks. "We'll be staying at a coaching inn this evening and shall depart tomorrow at dawn for Cairnwood Hall."

"You are welcome to stay at Rumney Manor for the evening," he offered.

"I think it's best if I leave after speaking to the girls," she admitted in a regretful tone. "I don't think my heart could bear more than one goodbye."

He started to offer his arm but stopped himself. He didn't trust himself to touch Emeline. For if he did, he doubted that he could refrain himself from pulling her into his arms.

"We'd best get this over with," he said gruffly as he started walking towards the estate.

Nothing was said between them as they made their way to the nursery. As they walked down the hall of the second level, he noticed that Emeline's steps faltered.

He stopped and turned to face her. "It will be all right," he tried to reassure her.

"I don't believe it will," she murmured.

Reaching out, he placed his hand on her sleeve. "This doesn't have to be a goodbye. If you so desire, you can write to the girls."

Her eyes snapped to his. "I would like that very much."

Dropping his arm, he walked to the door and opened it. He saw that Phoebe and Sophia were sitting quietly at their desks, and a young maid sat next to them.

Emeline brushed past him and moved towards the girls. They looked up at her in confusion.

"Why are you crying, Miss Wren?" Phoebe asked.

Sophia glanced over at him before whispering, "Did he fire you again?"

Emeline shook her head. "No, but I need to finish a story I told you earlier." She held out her hands and each girl eagerly latched on to one. She walked with them to the settee and sat down. The girls snuggled close to her.

The young maid excused herself from the room, and he closed the door behind her.

Emeline kissed both girls on the top of their heads.

"Do you remember the story about the girl that ran away from an evil stepmother and hid from her?" she asked.

Sophia nodded. "Yes. Emie worked as a governess for a handsome lord."

"Yes, that's the one. Emie loved her two charges, desperately." Her voice hitched. "But Emie's father came home from his business trip and discovered his daughter had run away."

"Was the father a good man?" Phoebe asked.

"Yes, a very good man," Emeline said. "The father searched everywhere for Emie, and he finally discovered her location."

"Did he come for her?" Sophia inquired.

Element smiled. "He did."

"I bet Emie was happy," Sophia remarked.

Her smile dimmed. "Emie was happy, but her heart was also sad."

Sophia scrunched her nose in confusion. "Why?"

"Because she knew she had to leave her charges behind."

Phoebe leaned back from Emeline, and there were tears in her eyes. "You're Emie, aren't you, Miss Wren?"

Emeline hesitated for a moment before admitting, "I am."

"You can't leave us!" Phoebe cried, jumping up from her seat. "You promised you would stay."

"I know, but my circumstances have changed."

Sophia looked up at her with wide eyes. "When are you leaving?"

"When we are finished with our little talk. I wanted to be sure I said goodbye to you."

"I will miss you," Sophia whimpered, throwing her arms around Emeline.

"I will miss you, too," she replied, closing her eyes.

"What are we going to do without you?" Phoebe asked.

Emeline gave her a tender smile. "You're lucky enough to have Lord Mountgarret to care for you. He will continue to shower love and affection on you."

Phoebe turned her gaze towards him. "Can you offer her more money to stay?"

Baldwin chuckled at her unexpected remark. "I already tried that."

"Lord Mountgarret gave me permission to write to you girls," Emeline said with emotion in her voice. "I expect to hear that you are both doing well in your lessons."

Both girls nodded with watery eyes and quivering chins.

Emeline turned her gaze towards Phoebe. "I want to hear all about how you are excelling in your riding lessons."

"I will," Phoebe answered.

Shifting her gaze towards Sophia, she said, "I know you dislike practicing your embroidery, but you must become proficient at it."

Sophia made a face. "I hate embroidery."

Emeline smiled. "You are sounding more like Phoebe every day."

Rising from her seat, she put her arms around the girls and pulled them in close. "I love you girls. Don't you ever forget that."

Baldwin felt tears prick his eyes as he watched the tearful scene before him.

After a long moment, Emeline dropped her arms and stepped back. "It's time for me to go."

Baldwin stepped forward and slipped an arm over each girls' shoulder. "I shall take care of them from here."

Her eyes filled with tears as she gave him an appreciative nod. "Thank you, Lord Mountgarret. Thank you for everything."

"You are welcome," he said.

Emeline stepped over and opened the door. "I will miss you, more than you will ever know," she said, waving at the girls.

The girls waved back, and they both murmured their goodbyes.

In the next moment, Emeline had disappeared through the door, closing it behind her. The girls started sobbing and leaned into him for support.

As he held the girls, he couldn't help but feel as though he was making a huge mistake letting Emeline go. But she couldn't stay on as the governess... not anymore. And he had no intention of offering for her again. He couldn't do that after she had blatantly lied to him.

So, he decided to let Emeline go, taking his heart with her.

The sun was barely rising when Baldwin raced his horse through the fields surrounding his property. He'd had a fitful night of sleep, and he couldn't seem to erase the hurt look on Emeline's face when he'd told her that he didn't trust her.

Which he didn't.

Not anymore.

She'd lied to him.

He'd revealed so much of himself to her, but she had hidden herself behind a mask of lies. How could he possibly trust her again? He already knew the answer. He couldn't. She had betrayed his trust, and there was no going back.

Last night had been awful. Phoebe and Sophia had cried for hours after Emeline had left. He knew it would take some time for the girls to adjust to a life without her. He'd spoken to Mrs. Garvey and was pleased to discover that she had received some inquiries about the governess position. He planned to interview the potential governesses himself to be sure that they were a good fit for the girls. However, he didn't think he would ever find someone as perfect for the girls... or him... as Emeline.

He reined in his horse in front of the pond that separated his and Penelope's lands. He dismounted and encouraged his horse to drink.

The last time he'd come to the pond, he'd been with Emeline, he realized. Would he always associate visiting the pond with her now? He hoped not.

A horse's whinny caught his attention, and he looked up. He was surprised to see Penelope and Nicholas on the other side of the pond, watching him with curious expressions.

"Are you all right, cousin?" Penelope asked, dismounting. "We have been calling your name."

"You have?" he asked.

Nicholas gave him a disapproving shake of his head. "If we'd been highway robbers, you would already be dead."

Baldwin rubbed his horse's neck. "I'm afraid I'm rather preoccupied this morning."

Penelope had a knowing look on her face. "Were you thinking about Emeline?"

"I was, in fact, but for an entirely different reason than you suppose."

Nicholas dismounted his horse. "What are you jabbering about?"

"Emeline is leaving for Cairnwood Hall this morning. She's going home."

A deep frown came to Penelope's lips. "What did you do, cousin?" Her tone was accusatory.

"I did nothing," he declared.

"Then why is she leaving?"

He shook his head. "It doesn't matter. She's leaving and it's for the best."

"For whom?" Nicholas asked. "Phoebe and Sophia loved Miss Wren."

He huffed. "That's the thing. There was no Miss Wren. She lied to me. Her real name was Miss Emeline Warren."

Nicholas shrugged. "So, she lied about her name. You banished her because of that?"

"I didn't *banish* her," Baldwin drawled. "Her father came to retrieve her."

"Did she tell you why she hid her identity?" Penelope asked, holding the reins loosely in her hands.

He looked at his cousin in surprise. "You knew she was lying about her name?"

"Of course, I did. She and I attended Miss Bell's Finishing School together," Penelope explained. "She asked me to keep her secret after she told me why she was hiding at Rumney Manor."

"Why didn't you tell me?" Baldwin shouted.

Penelope stood her ground. "It wasn't my place," she challenged.

"Emeline lied to me!"

Nicholas turned towards his wife. "May I ask why Miss Warren was concealing her identity?" he asked.

"Emeline's stepmother was cruel. She was attempting to force her into an arranged marriage to a man who was her father's age. When Emeline refused, the stepmother concocted a plan to lock her up in Bedlam while her father was away on business," Penelope shared.

"That seems rather harsh," Nicholas responded.

Penelope nodded. "I agree. She fled to Rumney Manor and accepted a position as the governess."

"It makes logical sense that she would hide her true identity under those circumstances. She was in danger," Nicholas replied.

"I believe so, as well," Penelope stated.

Baldwin looked at them in exasperation. "No, it does not make sense!" he exclaimed. "Everyone knows that only a male relation can send someone to Bedlam."

Penelope arched an eyebrow. "I wasn't aware of that fact."

"Regardless, she lied to me," Baldwin declared.

"For a good reason," Nicholas pressed.

"Is there ever a good reason to lie to someone?" he asked.

Nicholas let out a sigh. "You are angry with Miss Warren because she didn't tell you who she was from the very beginning."

"Yes."

"If I recall, you fired her after your first encounter with her," he said.

"That's true, but…"

Nicholas cut him off. "Have you thought that perhaps she didn't share her secret with you because she didn't trust *you*?"

"Regardless, she should have told me the truth."

Penelope shook her head. "I disagree."

"I beg your pardon?"

"Did Emeline tell you that I asked her to be my companion?" Penelope asked.

"No, she didn't."

"Do you want to know why she refused?"

"Why?"

Penelope lifted her brow. "Because she loved those girls. She would rather be a governess to them than be a companion."

Baldwin fisted the reins in his hand. "I don't doubt that she loved the girls, but..."

Nicholas interjected, "You are a fool to let her go without a fight."

"And why is that?" he asked dryly.

"Because with Miss Warren in your life, I find you to be a tolerable person," Nicholas said matter-of-factly.

"I'm sure that my cousin fought to keep Emeline with him at Rumney Manor," Penelope remarked, turning her gaze towards Baldwin. "Didn't you?"

"I did not," he admitted, shifting his gaze away from her. "I let her go."

"You let the best thing that has ever happened to you just walk out of your life... *willingly?*" Penelope asked, her voice rising. "Are you daft?"

"I told you. She lied to me," he defended.

"Balderdash, cousin," she proclaimed. "Everyone makes mistakes. After Nicholas saved me from that madman, I ran away from him because he was trying to force me into marriage. A marriage that I secretly wanted. But Nicholas came after me. He saved me... again."

"This is different," Baldwin claimed.

"You need to go after her," Penelope urged. "Go after her and beg for her forgiveness."

He shook his head. "It's too late. She's gone."

Nicholas stared at him, then asked, "Do you love her?"

"I do," Baldwin replied without hesitation.

"Then don't give up on her. Fight for her," Nicholas counseled.

"Even if I wanted to, I said some things that I can never take back," he shared. "I was so angry with her."

Penelope gave him a disapproving look. "Then it's best that you let her go. I want my friend to be happy, to be loved, and to feel the overwhelming joy of knowing that her love match will do anything to ensure her happiness." She gave him a weak smile. "I'm sad to know that man isn't you."

"I was supposed to be," he admitted, tilting his head back. "I even offered for her."

"What happened?" Penelope asked.

He ran a hand through his hair. "I took it back."

Nicholas stared incredulously at him. "You took it back?" he asked.

He nodded.

"He's past hope," Nicholas whispered to Penelope. "What's worse, I don't think he even recognizes that he just made the stupidest mistake of his life."

"No, he doesn't, but we must help him anyway," Penelope answered back.

"I don't think we can."

Baldwin cleared his throat. "You do realize that I can hear you over there."

Penelope looked over at him unashamed. "We're fully aware of that fact. We're just debating about how we can help you."

"What's the point?"

Nicholas met his gaze. "Life is entirely worth living when you find the one person that your heart connects with. It becomes filled with joy and happiness, filtering out all the pain of your past. It becomes meaningful." He frowned. "*That* is what you're giving up."

"And I am just supposed to start trusting her again."

"Yes!" Penelope and Nicholas shouted in unison.

"I am not sure I can," he reluctantly admitted.

"Then you don't deserve her, especially if you won't yield

because of your own stubborn pride," Nicholas responded. "Pride has no place in matters of the heart."

As Nicholas's words resonated in his mind, Baldwin realized that his friend was right. His own foolish pride had taken hold of him, causing him to send away the one person who had brought joy back into his life. He hung his head in shame.

"I'm a fool," he said humbly.

"I am not going to disagree with you there, cousin," Penelope stated.

"Even if I went after her, I don't believe she'll forgive me for the things I said."

"That is her choice," Penelope replied. "But do you think Emeline returns your affections?"

"I believe so," Baldwin said earnestly.

Nicholas waved his hand. "Then go! Go get Miss Warren back."

Knowing now what needed to be done, and not wanting to waste another moment, he placed his foot in the stirrup, mounted, and turned the reins to ride away.

Baldwin urged his horse faster as he raced back towards Rumney Manor. He had one chance to convince Emeline that he'd been wrong and plead for her to take him back. Would she forgive him after all the cruel things he'd said? He surely hoped so. For the thought of life without Emeline was too difficult to bear. He had to win her back! He just had to! He couldn't go back to a life without her.

17

STANDING NEXT TO THE COACH, THE SUN HAD BARELY RISEN AS Emeline stared down the cobblestone street in the town of Cadoxton. She hoped that Baldwin would come after her, to plead for her to stay with him, but it was all for naught. He wasn't coming. He had every right to be angry with her. She had lied to him, and she had to face those consequences.

"I don't think he's coming, do you, dear?"

She sighed. "I know, but I was hoping..." She stopped and tried to correct herself. "Who is coming, Father?"

Her father chuckled. "I'm not a simpleton, dear. You haven't been yourself since we left Rumney Manor."

"I miss Phoebe and Sophia."

"Just the girls?" he asked with a knowing look.

She forced a smile, despite the heartache she felt. "A part of me may miss Lord Mountgarret, as well."

"Come, let's go home," her father said, holding his hand out to her.

She slipped her hand into his and placed her foot onto the coach step. With one last parting glance at the empty street, she stepped into the coach and sat down on the bench. She took a moment and smoothed out her ivory skirt.

Her father stepped in and sat across from her. "I'm still amazed that you traveled with only three gowns to Rumney Manor."

"My clothing options were a little sparse," she admitted, "and I must admit that I'm looking forward to having a lady's maid again."

Her father's face grew serious. "I'm sorry that you were forced to flee from your home. It breaks my heart that I didn't know how miserable you truly were."

"I have felt so alone these past few years," she found herself sharing. "If it hadn't been for Harry and the rest of the household staff, I'm not sure how I would have gone on."

Her father's gaze shifted towards the window. "I truly believed that Priscilla would have been a good mother to you. After all, she had experienced loss, as well."

"She had?"

"You may remember my friend, Jerome Walters. He and I used to hunt together during the fox season."

Emeline nodded.

A flicker of sadness crept into her father's eyes. "About a year after your mother died, he died suddenly, leaving behind a wife and a young daughter. To make matters worse, he was heavily in debt and the bank repossessed the small estate the day after the funeral. The poor wife was tossed out onto the street, and she had to rely on her family's good graces for her support."

"That's awful."

"It was," he agreed. "When I heard about her plight, I decided that I could help her by offering for her hand in marriage. It seemed like it was a solution to both of our problems. You," he gestured, "would have a mother, and she would have stability in her life and for her daughter, Juliet."

"I had no idea."

Her father frowned. "I promise that Priscilla and I will have a serious talk when I get home."

Leaning forward in her seat, she reached for his hand. "It wasn't all terrible. I did attend nearly every ball, social gathering, and theatre performance in London during the Season. Priscilla was determined for me to marry."

"You were in London for three Seasons, and Priscilla informed me that you had received multiple offers."

"It's true," Emeline admitted, "but none of the offers appealed to me."

"May I ask why?" her father inquired, encompassing her hand in his.

She pondered his question for a moment before answering. "I was searching for something that none of those suitors had."

"Which was?"

An image of Baldwin came to her mind, but she quickly banished it. "It doesn't matter now."

"Doesn't it?"

She shook her head. "I think Priscilla was right. I filled my head with fantastical nonsense, and I need to stop reading fairy tales."

Her father sighed. "I can't help but wonder if you're leaving a part of your heart behind at Rumney Manor."

"I already told you, Father," she started, "nothing inappropriate happened between Lord Mountgarret and myself."

Watching her intently, he asked, "I believe you. But did *something* happen between you and Lord Mountgarret?"

Removing her hand from his, she brought it back to her lap. "Just before your arrival, Lord Mountgarret offered for me."

"He did?"

She bobbed her head.

"Did you accept?"

Shaking her head, she replied, "I did not."

"Why not?

"Because he proposed to Miss Wren, not to me," she admitted. "After I confessed who I truly was, he was furious."

"Oh dear," her father muttered.

"He told me that I'd lost his trust and said it would be best if I left," she revealed, lowering her gaze. "He hates me."

Her father shifted in his seat. "No, he doesn't hate you. He was just hurt."

"It is silly, really," she murmured, wiping at her eyes. "I've only known him for such a short time, but he's grown to mean so much to me." She laughed. "After our first meeting, he fired me for my impertinence."

Her father laughed. "I'm not surprised."

"When he attempted to rehire me, I refused unless he agreed to eat dinner with his two wards."

"That doesn't seem overly complicated."

She smiled. "You haven't had dinner with the girls. The first evening, Phoebe brought a frog to the table, and Lord Mountgarret had a fit."

"A frog?" He chuckled. "That sounds like something you would've done."

"After a few days, Lord Mountgarret bonded with the girls. He's even looking into adding a small pig farm to his property to make Phoebe happy."

"A *pig* farm?"

"Lord Mountgarret may come across as gruff, but he has a kind, loving heart," Emeline shared, turning her gaze towards the passing countryside in an attempt to hide her growing emotions. "He'll be good to those girls."

"I believe you," her father replied.

Tears came to her eyes, and she willed them to go away, but to her dismay, more slipped down her cheeks as she thought of what she'd left behind. Quickly, she swiped her cheeks with trembling fingertips.

Good heavens, what was wrong with her? She'd cried more

since coming to Rumney Manor than she had her entire life. What was the purpose of crying, anyway? It just proved that she was a simpering female. Besides, this was all her fault. She'd lied to the man who had stolen her heart.

"Oh, Emie," her father murmured as he placed a reassuring hand on her knee. "It will be all right."

"I apologize for my display of emotions," she said through a shaky breath.

"You don't ever need to apologize for showing emotion, my dear. It's what makes us human."

The coach jerked to the side, followed by the driver shouting. A moment later, the coach started to slow down.

"What do you suppose is going on out there?" her father asked as he turned his attention out the window.

"Do you think it's highwaymen?" Emeline asked, feeling frightened.

Her father didn't appear convinced. "I doubt it. We're still too close to town." He put his hand out the window and opened the door. "Stay here," he ordered before exiting the coach.

A second coach came to a stop next to them and the door opened. She gasped. It was Baldwin! He jumped out of his coach and approached her father. She couldn't hear what they were saying, but she saw her father gesturing wildly at him. A few more words were said, and her father stepped to the side.

Baldwin started to walk towards the coach, and she quickly closed the drapes. She didn't want him to think she'd been eavesdropping.

His voice came from outside of the window. "May I come in and speak to you?"

She paused, unsure how she should respond.

"Please, Emeline," he pleaded.

After only a moment, she responded, "All right."

Baldwin opened the door, entered the carriage, and sat across from her. "Don't leave me," he said, his eyes boring into hers.

"Please tell me that it's not too late, that I haven't lost you forever."

She stared at him in confusion. "I don't understand. I thought you hated me."

He leaned closer. "I was angry and hurt. Because of that, I spoke out of turn."

"I don't blame you. You had every right to be angry."

Reaching for Emeline's hands in her lap, he replied, "You're wrong. At the first test of my love, I failed you. I told you that I loved you, but then it was *I* who betrayed *you*." He brought her hands up to his lips. "I sent you away, believing it was for the best."

He watched her with longing in his brown eyes. "I'm not perfect. In fact, I am far from it. I work too much, criticize much too frequently, and I speak out of turn regularly. However, you make me a better man, a man worth knowing."

She smiled at him. "You're already one of the best men I know."

"I don't deserve your praise, not after what I said to you," he sighed. "I need your help, Emeline. The girls…"

"Need a mother?" she repeated. "Haven't we already had this discussion?"

He nodded. "Yes, but they *do* need a mother. However, that's not why I need your help." His eyes now turned pleading. "I need you in my life. I need your eternal optimism. I need you to challenge me, to love me. I want to marry you, because I can't live without you. You see, I've fallen hopelessly, desperately, in love with you, and it scares me."

"Why is that?"

"Because I'm afraid I won't be the man that you need, and I am so frightened of losing you." He tightened his hold on her hands. "What do you say, Emie?"

She looked at him in surprise. "You called me Emie."

"I did," he said, looking unsure of himself. "Is that all right?"

"It is," she replied, smiling. "I find I prefer that over Miss Wren."

He returned her smile. "Will you marry me?"

"Yes," she breathed.

"We will post the banns tomorrow and marry in three weeks." He leaned closer, a small smile tugging on his lips. "That will give me three weeks to court you properly."

"You truly wish to court me?"

"I do, very much," he replied. "I wish to take you on carriage rides, bring you flowers, and sneak a kiss in the gardens."

"I think that sounds wonderful…"

Before she finished her thought, he captured her lips with his. The kiss was long, slow, and achingly sweet. It was a kiss filled with the assurance of a shared future.

"Emie," he murmured against her lips, "my love. I promise I will try to live up to your belief in me."

"You already have. You came after me," she replied before she initiated another kiss.

After a delightful moment, Baldwin leaned back. "I hope, with time, you'll grow to love me as much as I love you."

She placed her hand on his right cheek. "I already do love you, Baldwin."

"You do?"

"I do, completely," she whispered.

Baldwin pressed his lips against hers, but this time was different. It was hard, unyielding, then he deepened the kiss, making it even more perfect.

A clearing of the throat came from outside of the coach. "Need I remind you, Lord Mountgarret, that you are not alone," her father stated in a warning tone.

"Right," Baldwin said as he leaned back. "I nearly forgot that I brought two stowaways with me."

"Stowaways?" she repeated, her smile growing. She already had an idea who these stowaways were.

"Would you care to see them?" he asked, opening the door.

The door was barely open when Phoebe and Sophia jumped into the coach and wrapped their arms around her. "Miss Warren!" they shouted.

"I see that Lord Mountgarret informed you of my real name." Sophia's arms tightened around her. "Yes. We practiced it while our coach was chasing yours down."

Phoebe leaned back and asked in an eager voice, "Did you say yes? Are you going to be our new mother?"

"I am," she announced enthusiastically.

Both girls cheered before Phoebe whispered, "Did he have to beg?"

"Only a little," Emeline whispered back, offering Baldwin a private smile.

Reaching out, Baldwin closed the door to the coach and asked, "Are you ready to go home?"

Home.

Why did that word sound so enticing?

"Yes, I am," she replied as the coach began moving. "But what about my father?"

"He has stepped into my coach and is following us back to Rumney Manor," Baldwin shared. "He will stay at my estate until we are wed."

"Truly?"

Baldwin nodded. "Your father said he wanted to get to know his new granddaughters before the wedding."

As her arms tightened around the girls, Emeline realized that everything that she had ever hoped for was in this coach. She had the man of her dreams, two adorable girls, and a home that would be filled with love.

Her fairytale dreams had come true.

EPILOGUE

ONE YEAR LATER

SITTING ON A BLANKET IN THE GRASS, EMELINE HELD HER ONE-month-old baby, James, tightly in her arms as she watched Baldwin crouch down next to the stream in the woodlands.

"I got one," he announced proudly as he held up a large bullfrog.

"It's about time!" Phoebe declared, sitting near him on a rock. "We've been out here for nearly an hour."

Baldwin chuckled as he released the frog back into the stream. "I'm afraid I am not as practiced as you are at scooping up frogs."

Coming to sit next to her, Sophia moved the blanket near James's face to get a closer look at him.

"He sure does sleep a lot," she complained.

"That's what babies do."

Sophia looked up at her. "When do you think James will be able to play hide and seek with me?"

"Not for a few years, at least."

Sophia blew out a puff of air. "What's the point of having a baby brother if he can't play with me?"

"Don't worry, in a few years, you will be begging for him to leave you alone," Emeline promised.

"I doubt that."

Emeline smiled as she heard a pig snorting in the distance. Phoebe jumped up from the rock. "Can Sophia and I go visit the piglets?"

Baldwin wiped his hands on his trousers. "I suppose so, but this time don't get so close to the pig enclosure."

Phoebe placed a hand on her hip and declared, "It wasn't my fault last time. The mud was slippery, and we fell in."

"Yes, and you ruined two dresses in the process," Baldwin chided lightly.

Sophia rose from the blanket. "We'll be better, Father."

Baldwin smiled tenderly down at Sophia. "I know you will, my dear. That's why I love you as much as I do."

"Come on, Sophia," Phoebe encouraged as she turned to run down the path towards the pig farm.

As they watched the girls disappear into the cover of the trees, Baldwin came to sit next to her.

"How do you like the girls calling you Father?" Emeline asked curiously.

His eyes filled with tears. "It's an honor I scarcely deserve." He turned his gaze towards her. "They've been calling you Mother for nearly six months, but they only just started calling me Father."

"I knew it was only a matter of time," she said, leaning into his shoulder. "They adore you."

"And I them." He leaned down and kissed her lips. "Are you happy, my dear?"

She smiled. "You ask me that all the time."

"I know. I just want to ensure that you are happy."

"I am, blissfully so." She shifted the baby in her arms. "And are you?"

"Happy?" he asked. "How can I not be? I have the perfect wife and three wonderful children. I truly never thought it was possible to be this happy."

"That pleases me."

Baldwin rose and dusted off his trousers. "Come, we'd better hurry if we want to arrive at Cairnwood Hall before dark."

"Do we have to?" she asked, glancing down at the sleeping babe.

He held out his hand to help her rise. "Your stepsister's engagement ball is tonight."

"Oh yes, how can I forget?" she joked. "She landed herself a duke."

"Are you jealous?"

She chuckled as she rose. "Not particularly, considering the Duke of Sommerset is eighty years old."

Baldwin grinned. "Is he that young? I thought he was older."

Once she was on her feet, Baldwin placed his hand at the base of her neck and kissed her soundly.

"I love you," he murmured against her lips.

"I love you, too."

He glanced down at the baby, his eyes lingering. "I can't believe we created something so perfect." His voice hitched with emotion. "Thank you for never giving up on me. I know I don't deserve your love."

"You're wrong. Besides, I love you more every day," she assured him.

He gave her a boyish grin. "So, where do we go from here, Emie?"

"Anywhere we want to," she paused, "as long as we're together."

"That sounds perfect, because I never plan to let you go."

"You promise?"

He slipped his arm around her shoulder and leaned in.

"Always and forever," he murmured in her ear. "Always and forever."

The End

ABOUT THE AUTHOR

Laura Beers is an award-winning author. She attended Brigham Young University, earning a Bachelor of Science degree in Construction Management. She can't sing, doesn't dance and loves naps.

Besides being a full-time homemaker to her three kids, she loves waterskiing, hiking, and drinking Dr. Pepper. She was born and raised in Southern California, but she now resides in South Carolina.

Printed in Great Britain
by Amazon